Bringing Up
Good Parents &
Other Jobs for
Teenage Girls

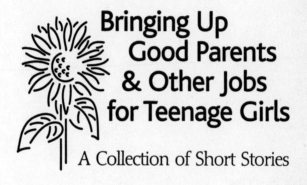

Bringing Up
Good Parents
& Other Jobs
for Teenage Girls

A Collection of Short Stories

Nancy Rue

VINE
BOOKS

SERVANT PUBLICATIONS
ANN ARBOR, MICHIGAN

© 2001 by Nancy Rue
All rights reserved.

Vine books is an imprint of Servant Publications especially designed to serve evangelical Christians.

Published in association with the literary agency of Alive Communications, Inc., 7680 Goddard St., Suite 200, Colorado Springs, CO 80920.

Published by Servant Publications
P.O. Box 8617
Ann Arbor, Michigan 48107

Cover design: Uttley/DouPonce DesignWorks, Sisters, Oregon

01 02 03 04 10 9 8 7 6 5 4 3 2 1

Printed in the United States of America
ISBN 1-56955-230-4

For Kelly Gordon
who has finished all the teenage jobs
and is now a wonderful young woman.

CONTENTS

Dear Girlfriends,

Whenever I write a short story, I try to imagine that I'm telling the story to a group of girls I'm sitting around painting toenails with. In between the "Could you pass me the Romantic Red?" and the "Uh, is your mom gonna mind that I just dumped nail polish remover on the rug?" we're sharing something that happened to somebody, something that affected her life in some way. And what do girls hanging out doing pedicures talk about more than how HARD it is to be a teenage female?

Seriously, don't you sometimes feel like this is the toughest thing you've ever done, being adolescent? I still grit my teeth when I hear somebody say to a fifteen-year-old girl, "These are the best years of your life. Enjoy them!" Yeah, there's a lot of fun to be had, and a lot of things are brand new to you, which can be exciting. But don't let anybody try to tell you life doesn't get any better than this. That's the last thing you want to hear when you'd swear everything is falling apart!

There's the whole relationship thing—boys, good friends, not-so-good friends, parents. Then you've got to figure out who you are and try to be that while everybody else seems content to be who everybody else is. And, of course, you have to deal with school and responsibilities and the ever-hovering question of what you are going to do with your life. If these are the "best years," I wouldn't blame you if what you did with your life was pull a bag over your head!

That's why these stories I've told while we've painted our toenails together are simply the stories of girls who have faced what you're facing and have figured out how God helps. I hope as you meet Brittany, Chrissy, Cherise, and the rest, you'll break out the nail polish, get to know them, and find some things that entertain you—'cause what good is a story unless you can get into it? I hope these stories will give you some insights for dealing with the issues in your own life as well.

You'll notice that in the last section, "It Must Be So Easy Being a Guy," the ones telling the stories are Andy, Shaun, and Ben—boys. I've included them because, while a guy wouldn't be caught dead reading a story with a female main character, the girls I've talked to like to try to see things from the guy-perspective. If you ask me, I think it would be a better world if guys saw things from the girl-perspective, too, but that's beside the point! I just hope you'll find some things in their tales that enlighten you about the male mystery.

The way I see it, you need all the help you can get if you're going to complete the job of being an adolescent female and come out knowing who you are, where you're going, how to deal with other people while you're on the way, and—most important of all—how God works through it all. So get out the Crashing Coral and the emery boards and meet Jen and Samantha and Walker. I'll be praying for you and for a job well done!

Nancy Rue

Today,
I Think
I'll Save
the World

My Tapestry Is Unraveling

Like usual, I was at my grandmother's after school. Like usual, she was sitting listlessly at the kitchen table, dabbing at her eyes with a Kleenex, and, like usual, I was attempting to get her mind on something besides the fact that my grandfather had died two months earlier and he *wasn't* coming back.

"Granna, come on," I said. "Just go to the mall with me. You used to love to shop."

"I loved to buy clothes for your grandpa," she said, gazing out the window with empty eyes.

"So buy something for yourself."

"And where would I wear it? Everywhere I go reminds me of him."

I tried not to laugh. "Then buy something for *me.*"

Her eyes drifted from the window to me. "You have plenty of places to go, don't you, Brittany?" she said. "You have your whole life ahead of you. Mine's all behind me."

I tried not to groan as her eyes misted up again. I didn't see how she could have any tears *left.*

"Get my purse, Honey," she said. "I'll give you some money

to buy yourself something nice to wear out someplace."

"No, Granna!" I wailed. "I want you to go with me! That's the whole idea—to get you out of the house."

Like usual, she pursed her mouth so the wrinkles feathered around her lips, and, like usual, I was about as frustrated as I knew how to be. Lucky for both of us the phone rang.

"You get it," she said, eyes going empty again. "Tell them I can't talk right now."

They already know that, I thought. *I'm surprised anybody's calling—you tell them that every time.*

It was my best friend, Elizabeth. Her voice was breathless and weak.

"What's wrong?" I said.

"They're at it again. Can you meet me?"

"Where?"

"At the 7-Eleven."

"What's going on?"

"I can't talk. Just meet me."

Actually, she didn't have to tell me. I knew the scene by heart. I kissed Granna and made her promise to eat the Hamburger Helper I'd whipped up for her dinner, then took off for the 7-Eleven on the corner. The Elizabeth Story played in my head.

"They hate me. I know they hate me," she always said when her parents went into one of their rage-duets. "Why else would they treat me this way?"

"Because alcohol does weird stuff to people," I would always tell her.

"How would you know?" she'd say. "Your parents are perfect!"

Then I'd remind her that since she'd told me her parents both had drinking problems, I'd done a bunch of reading about it. I'd tell her—again—what I'd read and what it said she should do, and I'd help her find a way to get back home and to try again to live with her parents.

What I never told her was that my parents *weren't* perfect. They had problems of their own that were fast becoming *my* problems.

But I erased those when I saw Elizabeth standing outside the phone booth, face swollen from crying. I'd seen her look that way about a hundred times, and, like usual, I went up and put my arms around her. Like usual, she sobbed into my shoulder.

"My dad didn't even go to work today," she said between hiccups. "He's been drinking all day. My mom came home and started yelling at him, and then she had to have a drink to calm down, and then they *both* started hollering at me." She pulled away and blinked into my face. "They told me I'm a tramp because I want to go out with Kevin—just because he's two years older than I am."

"They don't even know what they're saying, remember? You can't reason with them when they're drunk."

"So what do I do?"

I sighed and held back the we-have-been-through-this-a-thousand-times speech. "You get out of the situation until they sober up and then tell them how much their drinking is hurting you."

"It doesn't work!" she said. She shook her head like one of those figurines you put on your dashboard.

"OK," I said. "Do you want to come home with me?"

"I don't know. It seems like I'm always doing that."

"It's better than getting slapped or something. My parents don't mind."

She wiped the tears off her cheeks with the back of her hands and shook her head. "I called Kevin, too, and he said he'd meet me here in half an hour. I just didn't want to wait alone. That's why I called you."

"Call me again if you need me," I said. "I'll be home. I have to write that paper."

A Toyota pickup roared into the parking space in front of us, and Elizabeth squeezed my hand. "Thanks, Britt," she said. "I love you."

"Love you, too," I said. Like usual, I watched her go with a sinking stomach. I'd stake my G.P.A. on the fact that she wouldn't go to her parents when they sobered up. It would just start all over again like a song you hate, set on repeat.

Like my life is that much different, I thought as I trudged toward my house, a few blocks down. Lately it seemed like the same old thing was going on there, too.

My parents didn't drink or fight. They just didn't speak to each other anymore. When it had started, I couldn't say. I'd only begun to notice it when my grades had started falling.

"What's this C in English?" Mom said to me one night.

Dad looked up from his latest issue of *Time* and said, "You got a C in English? What's that about?"

"I just can't concentrate," I said.

"That's easy to understand." Dad folded a crease into the magazine that, surprisingly, didn't rip the pages.

"*I* don't understand it," Mom said to me.

"It's this tension around here, isn't it, Britt?" Dad said—again, to me.

"It *is* hard to do my schoolwork when I'm so stressed out."

"That isn't my fault, Brittany," Mom said. "Talk to your father about that."

"No," Dad said, slapping the *Time* onto the coffee table. "Talk to your mother. But good luck getting her to answer you."

"I will talk to *you*, Brittany," she said. "You're a rational human being."

At that point Dad stormed out of the room, and the usual silence descended once again.

But this day when I opened the front door, they were definitely talking. On their highest volume settings.

"So that's your solution?" Mom was shouting. "You're just going to run away?"

"I'm not running away, Debbie. I'm trying to save my sanity."

"You're saying I'm driving you crazy."

"I'm saying I need some breathing space. We both do. The situation here is intolerable for everybody."

It was then that he noticed me standing in the doorway, and it was then that I noticed the bulging duffel bag by his feet. He looked at me sadly and picked it up.

"I won't be far away," he said—to me, not to Mom. "I'll let you know which hotel I'm at."

"You're *leaving*?" I said. My heart was pounding right up out of my throat. "Dad, no! That isn't right! You could get marriage counseling or something."

"Staying here sniping at your mother isn't right either," he said. His voice had fallen to a softer level, and there was a mist in his eyes as he leaned down to kiss me on the cheek. He looked so much like his mother—sad and empty and hopeless—that I started crying, too.

But he left anyway and left Mom in no mood to discuss it.

"It isn't about you, Brittany," she said when I begged her to tell me what was going on. "I just need some time alone. Don't you have a paper to write?"

"Yes, but, Mom, how can I ..."

"When is it due?"

"Day after tomorrow, but ..."

"Then you'd better get to it. You don't need any more Cs. You're an A student. We—*I* expect more of you."

Good grief, I thought, as I made my way upstairs. *She's already talking like a single parent. What am I going to do about this?*

What was I going to do about anything, for that matter? I felt strangely like some kind of tapestry, unraveling one thread at a time. But I couldn't worry about *me*—I had to do something to help *them*.

What I did was not even look at my notecards on Charles Dickens. Instead I got out my journal and wrote and wrote and wrote. That was how I always talked to God. I knew if I just kept pouring out my soul and what was coming to me, I'd figure out what to do.

Finally, I knew. I broke out my Bible and wrote two long letters—one to my father and one to my mother.

"You can't get a divorce," I told them. "Listen to what the Bible says about that." Then I listed every Scripture I could find on the subject, and then I promised I would do everything I could to make life easier for them at home so they could work out their problems. If that included making straight As, then I'd make A-pluses.

By the time I finished it was 10 P.M. I looked wearily at the stack of notecards and tried to drum up some energy to get started. If I was going to make promises like that, I was going to have to follow through, or their whole marriage could fall apart.

No sooner had I reached for everything-you-always-wanted-to-know-about-19th-century-British literature than the phone rang. It was Elizabeth.

She was crying so hard I could barely understand her.

"It's horrible!" she said—I think. "She threw the iron at me ..."

"You have to get out of there!" I said. "Just run here, as fast as you can."

We hung up without good-byes, and I ran down to find my mother, who was scrubbing the kitchen floor.

"That was Elizabeth," I said. "It's really bad over there. Can she ..."

"Not this time," she said. She sat back on her heels and squeezed the rag into the bucket as if getting rid of dirty water was the most important task of her life. "I can't handle anything else right now."

I stared. "But Mom! She can't stay there; it's dangerous!"

"I'm really sorry," Mom said woodenly. "I really am. But there must be someplace else. I would be no good to Elizabeth tonight."

For the first time I heard the catch in her voice, and I knew she was about to cry. As I stormed out the front door, it was beyond me how she could think of herself at a time like this. *You have to put your own stuff aside when somebody else needs you,* I told her in my mind. *That's what I do.*

I met Elizabeth at the corner and steered her down toward Granna's house. In all the times I'd rescued her, I'd never seen her cry that hard.

I got her onto the porch, where she sank onto the swing while I knocked on the door. And then pounded. And then jammed my thumb into the doorbell about twenty times and yelled, "Granna" through the window until I was hoarse.

If I'd thought my tapestry was unraveling before, it was in shreds by now.

"What in the world?" I said. "Why won't she answer the door?"

Elizabeth just shook her head and kept crying.

"OK," I said. "I'm gonna try the window."

It was locked, of course, so I jumped down into the shrubbery and looked around for a stick to pry it open. That's where I was when I heard Elizabeth scream.

"What's wrong?" I said.

I knew the minute I straightened up. A police car was just coming to a stop in front of the house, its blue lights twirling eerily in the dark.

"They sent the cops for me!" Elizabeth cried. Where she went or how she got there, I couldn't tell you. She just disappeared, leaving me standing in my grandmother's gardenia bushes facing a policeman who was approaching me with one hand on his gun and the other held up in warning.

"Don't move," he said.

"I won't," I said, although it was hard not to collapse into the mulch.

"What are you doing?" he said.

I told him—somehow. He looked at me for a good thirty seconds before he gave me a hand to pull me out of the bushes. "Anybody we can call to let us in to check on your grandmother?" he said.

"My dad," I said. And then a little more of me unraveled. I had no idea where he was.

It took us half an hour to find him at his hotel and convince him that this really was an emergency.

Nobody else seemed to think that except me, and I was right. When Dad finally got there with the key, we found Granna in her bed—unconscious. On her bedside table was an empty container of amitriptyline.

"Anti-depressant," Dad told the policeman. "The doctor said it was safe."

"Not if you take the whole bottle," the cop said. He radioed for an ambulance.

From there on I was coming apart in whole tapestry sections at once. By the time the ambulance screamed away with Dad in the front and Granna lying motionless in the back, I couldn't even stand up anymore. I sank down on Granna's bed, looked up at the ceiling, and said, "God! What good does it do to try to help all these people? I give up, God. Do You hear me? I just give up. You do it!"

Then the strangest thing happened. Instead of feeling the last thread loose itself from my Brittany-tapestry, I just felt, I don't know, calm somehow. So calm, in fact, that I fell asleep right there.

I didn't wake up until Elizabeth made her way into my grandmother's unlocked house. She found me in the bedroom and shook me. There was sunlight slanting in through the blinds and into my eyes.

"What's going on?" I said, squinting at her.

"You better get home," she said. "I went by your house this morning to get you for school, and your mom's in a panic because you didn't come home last night. Are you OK?"

"Yeah," I said. I looked around for my shoes, which, it turned out, were still on my feet.

She sat down on the bed beside me. "I'm not. It was so awful when I had to go home last night, Britt. My dad was pacing around the house like some animal in a cage. And my mom ..."

Like usual, I started to go into my litany with her, but the thought I'd gone to sleep with tripped me up.

"Stop, Liz," I said.

She did, out of sheer shock, I'm sure.

"Look," I said. "I hate it that everything is a mess at your house. Believe me, I know what it's like."

"You do not."

"Yeah, well, we'll go into that later. Just believe me when I say all I can do for you right now is keep praying. But I have to give you to God. I can't do anything else."

She sat there, mouth hanging halfway open, while I got up and smoothed out Granna's covers.

"What am I supposed to do?" she asked.

"What I've told you a bajillion times," I said.

"What are *you* gonna do?"

"Go find out about my grandmother. After that, I have no idea."

When I got home, Mom had one of those motherly two-emotions-at-the-same-time things going on. She grabbed me like I'd been gone six months, but her eyes were blazing.

"How's Granna?" I said.

"Your dad just called. They brought her around, and she said she just couldn't go on without Harry so she took all the pills. She'll be fine physically, but she's giving everyone a hard time, saying she wants to die too. Your dad thought if you came over and talked to her ..."

"I can't," I said. "There isn't anything more I can say to her. I have to get ready for school."

Mom shook her head. "It's been an awful night, Britt. Why don't you stay home today?"

I nodded and proceeded to my room like I was made of lead. Gone was the peaceful feeling I'd had the night before, and in its place was this sense of being completely useless. I hadn't helped Granna at all—she'd tried to commit suicide, for Pete's sake. I hadn't done a thing for Mom and Dad. Mom certainly wasn't rushing to the hospital to be at her husband's side. And then there was Elizabeth: She was probably running around right now, looking for another place to stay, instead of going home. I hadn't fixed a single one of them, for all my trying, and the only thing that had brought me any peace was giving up.

I slumped into my desk chair but I couldn't quite get my hand to reach for my journal. "God?" I said out loud, "What do I do now?"

Mom went on to work and I tried to go to sleep, but two things kept me awake. One was the unanswered question. The other, weirdly enough, was the stack of notecards on my desk.

How can I even think about doing a paper at a time like this?
I asked myself.

But, not at *all* like usual, I went to the computer and flipped through the cards and started typing, one painstaking line at a time.

Once in a while my mind darted to Elizabeth, Granna, or my parents. But every time, I came back to the same conclusion— "I've done all I can. What do I do now, God?"—and then I'd keep typing.

By 3 P.M., the paper was done. It wasn't a masterpiece, but it was definitely better than anything else I'd turned out that semester. I was printing it when the phone rang. It was, like usual, Elizabeth. Only she wasn't sobbing into the receiver.

"I went to see Mr. Sheetz," she said.

"The counselor?"

"Yeah. He signed me up to go to Al-Anon. There's a meeting third period tomorrow. I get out of class to go. That's how important he says it is. I don't know, though."

"What do you mean you don't know?"

"What do I need a group for when I have you?" she said.

"Go," I said. "Those people know what they're doing. I don't think I really do when it comes to having parents who drink."

"Are you saying you won't help me anymore?" Elizabeth's voice was going up into a whine.

"No," I said. "I'm praying for you. I'll always listen. But ..."

"Fine," she said. "See ya later."

Not at all like usual, I hung up the phone feeling as if I'd actually done something for her.

I liked the feeling so much that I went back to my room and

tore up the two letters I'd written to my parents. I was curled up on my window seat, praying for Granna, when Dad tapped on my door. I practically threw myself into his arms.

"She's gonna be OK," he said into my hair. "Thirty days in the hospital and then some ongoing psychiatric help. The docs say she's severely depressed."

I pushed back from him. "Good," I said. "I mean about the psychiatric help."

"Good?" he asked. He shook his head, eyes all guilty. "I was so wrapped up in my own stuff I didn't even see how bad off she was. I could have prevented this."

"You know what, Dad?" I asked. "We all have to stop trying to fix each other."

He gave a hard laugh. "What do you suggest we do then, Brittany? Hang around and wait for the answers to fall out of the sky?"

I started to roll my eyes at him, but I stopped. Waiting for the answers to fall out of the sky was exactly what I'd been doing all day, and I suddenly realized that I was starting to weave back together, thread by thread, as a result.

Of course, I wasn't sure Dad would get that, so I said, "We can get people the help they need, for starters."

He glowered at me. "Don't start with me about marriage counseling."

"OK," I said. "If you don't want to hear it, I won't. I'll just pray."

His frown got confused, in a way that told me that even as he left my room shaking his head, I'd maybe planted a seed.

Like usual, I wanted to run after him and try to make it all right. But like brand-new-usual, I closed the door behind him and went back to my window seat and prayed again.

"God," I said. "Thanks for unraveling me enough to get rid of that one bad thread—the one that said, 'It's all up to you, Brittany. It's all up to you.'"

20/20

O K. Where are you, you little piece of slime? Come on! I haven't got all night ..." I slid my hand cautiously across what I *thought* was the carpet. I couldn't see a thing without my contacts. "Oh, man—where are you? This isn't fun anymore."

"Who are you talking to, Chrissy?"

My little sister. I shot my hand out behind me. "Don't move, Tasha. You'll step on my contact!"

"I don't walk on the dresser," she said.

"Is it on the dresser?" I asked through my teeth.

"Yup."

"Hand it to me, please."

She did, and I stuck the lens in my mouth and then in my eye.

"Mama says spit's not good for those," Tasha said, settling down on my bed as if she'd been invited.

I ignored her as I popped the other lens in and blinked the world into focus.

"What are you getting all dressed up for?" she said.

"Party."

"Where?"

"Shelby's."

"Who's she?"

"Somebody I used to know."

"Before Daddy was a missionary? Before you went to Bolivia?"

"Yep."

"I didn't know anybody before we went to Bolivia."

"Of course you didn't. You were born there."

"But I'm still American."

That's funny, I thought bitterly as I stuck in an earring. *I actually lived here in Houston once, and I don't feel like an American.*

"Why aren't you smiling?" Tasha asked. "Don't you want to go to the party?"

I picked up my Birkenstocks. "I want to go."

"Why?"

"Because I saw Shelby at the mall today and she remembered me and she invited me."

What I didn't add as I buckled my Birkeys was that Shelby had remembered me *after* I had had to practically administer shock treatment to jog her memory. I could still see the scene in my head. She'd been coming out of Dillard's department store, shouting good-bye to somebody, and I recognized her voice. She always sounded like one of the Chipmunks on fast forward.

"Shelby?" I had said.

She'd stared at me as if I'd just materialized from the Starship Enterprise. "Yeah?" she'd said warily.

"It's me—Christina—Chrissy Trice. Remember? Fourth grade?"

"Chrissy!" she'd screamed.

"Psych!" I said.

Another blank stare.

"Don't you remember when we used to say that to each other?" I'd asked.

Evidently she hadn't, but that didn't keep her from hugging me and screaming some more. "This is so rad that I ran into you today! I mean, whoa, this is freaking me out—first I get my license …"

"You got your license?"

"My learner's permit—I'm fifteen and a half today. Do you have yours yet?"

"No. In Bolivia you have to be twenty-one to drive, unless you pay somebody off, of course, but …"

My voice had trailed off as I remembered with an ache that it didn't matter anymore what they did in Bolivia. I wasn't going back. Daddy was retiring from the mission field. My life there was over. I'd never see Darinka or Eduardo or any of them again.

"So—will you come?"

Shelby had looked expectantly at me.

"Come where?" I'd asked.

"Are you a schizoid? To my celebration party?"

I'd just nodded at her. I'd been halfway between missing Darinka and Eduardo and wondering what a schizoid was.

Now as I looked in the bedroom mirror and fingered the earrings Darinka and Eduardo had helped me pick out in

Cochabamba, I didn't feel any closer to either them or the schizoids here. No wonder I wasn't smiling.

"I'm not going to go," I muttered.

"Why?" Tasha said.

"Never mind." I left to tell Dad I wouldn't need a ride. He was out on the deck, contentedly playing with his telescope.

"You ready to go, Sweetie?" he said.

"No," I said. "I changed my mind."

He gave me one of those looks that opens a hole in my head, sees what I'm thinking, and cuts to the chase.

"Did you promise you'd go?" he said.

"Yes."

"Then I'll get my keys and meet you out in front. We can talk about it in the car."

He squeezed my shoulder and went into the house.

I sighed and looked into his telescope. "I wish this thing could see all the way to Bolivia," I whispered to myself. "Then I could see what Eduardo and Darinka are doing."

But I already knew. Eduardo was getting ready to go to Paraguay to work in a mission training program and Darinka was probably packing to be an exchange student.

Even if I did go back to Bolivia, nothing would be the same there either, I thought. The horn blew, and I walked out to the car.

"I've learned that wherever you are, Christina," my father said as we cruised toward Shelby's, "that's where God wants you right then."

"That doesn't really help much, Daddy," I said, trying *not* to sound as if I were willing to leap from the moving vehicle to avoid a lecture. "I need a *place.*"

"God will give you your place."

"But I feel totally out of it!"

"Then that must be your place," he said.

"You're telling me 'totally out of it' is my place?"

He pulled up in front of Shelby's and blinked at me through his glasses. "That's what I'm telling you. That smile will come back soon. Have a good time, Sweetie."

When Shelby met me at the door, she looked at me *again* as if I'd arrived via transporter, and when her synapses did connect she yelled, "Chrissy's here!" I could hear somebody behind her saying, "Who?"

She let me in and then immediately ran squealing into the kitchen with two other girls. The ones she left behind in the living room mumbled their names to me. None of the three boys did. When the girls went back to examining Shelby's priceless learner's permit, I sat there feeling like a package of Kotex on the cereal shelf and amused myself by making up names for the guys. Thrasher. El-Pimple-o. Mr. Head-in-the-History-Book. Mr. Head wore Coke-bottle glasses and didn't say a word. The other two never shut up, although the girls told them to at ten-second intervals.

At a party in Bolivia, I thought miserably, *I'd be surrounded by brown faces with laughing black eyes, and we'd be talking about our street ministry.* I shook my head. This could not *possibly* be my place.

"What's wrong?" Shelby said. "Don't you want to play Twister?"

"What?" I said.

She called out, "Left foot blue!"

That was the cue for everybody except Mr. Head-in-the-History-Book to scream. In about five minutes everyone in the room was tangled up like a bunch of paper clips on the large plastic sheet, still shrieking. Everyone, that is, except for Mr. Head and me.

"What about her—the new—what's your name again?"

"Christina," I said pointedly to the red-faced girl who was looking at me upside down between El Pimple-o's knees.

"Come on, play!" she said.

Somebody else yelled "Right foot green!"

I looked doubtfully at the snarl of people. I knew that if I really said no to Twister they'd immediately forget I was even there. Maybe that was why I gingerly stuck my foot onto a green dot. But then they yelled, "Right hand red!" and as I reached across some girl's butt for the red space I felt four people topple over underneath me. Two more piled on top of me. One deadened my eardrum.

"Shelby! The pizza is here!" an adult voice cried above the din.

Everyone emptied from the room like a bunch of jelly beans exiting the bag. In the process, both of my contacts popped out.

"I don't believe this," I said out loud. I was talking to myself. It was the first time I'd felt safe speaking since I'd gotten there.

I squatted and ran my hands across the Twister sheet. "They're probably stuck to the bottom of somebody's Nike," I said. "If anybody even wears Nikes anymore."

"Can I help?" said a male voice from the doorway.

I squinted in the direction of a blur whose only distinguishing feature was height. A tall boy with a civilized voice. Anything else and I'd have thrown one of my Birkeys at him. It had to be Shelby's older brother. What was his name? Rats—was it Kevin? Brian?

"Lose your contacts?" he said.

"Yeah," I said. "And my mind."

I could hear him running his palm across the rug. "What makes you say that?"

"Because I was nuts to come here. I should have known better."

"They say hindsight is 20/20."

"I think foresight is, too," I said, digging into rug fibers with my fingers. "I *know* what the future holds for me."

"What?" he said.

I almost didn't answer, but I'd just spent an hour with a cage full of orangutans, and he sounded like something farther up on the food chain.

"Being totally lost, having no idea what anybody is talking about, having a whole different idea of fun than everybody else my age." I sat up on my heels and gazed at his blur. "I was right there in the room with all of them, but there might as well still have been a whole ocean between us for as well as I fit in."

"Oh, yeah. Shelby said you were on the mission field. Did you like Bolivia?"

"I loved it."

"Then why don't you go back—like when you graduate?"

I felt that ache again. "It wouldn't be the same," I said. "I just wish I could see right *now* as clearly as I can see behind me and ahead of me. What do you call that—nowsight?"

"What *do* you see now?" he said.

I closed my eyes. Tears were threatening to spill over. "I see that I no longer belong in the world where I feel at home, and I don't feel at home in the world where I supposedly belong. My father says where you are is where God wants you to be, but where I am is ..." I stopped and swallowed. "Depressed," I said, and went back to the floor. I felt like an idiot.

There was a long silence, and I thought he'd escaped. But then he said. "Insight."

"What?"

"There's hindsight and foresight. I think what you see about the present is insight."

I squinted at him. "I thought insight was something really profound."

"What you said was pretty profound. I mean, I hear you, believe me—you don't exactly blend around here. But that's because you're way ahead of most of us. You've been out winning souls for the Lord. We've been trying to win dates for the prom." He paused. "Still, they all admire you or they wouldn't have been showing off so much tonight. Shelby told us we had to try to make a good impression because you were, like, 'way more ma*chur!*'"

I snorted, but it made me stop pawing the rug and think. "So, what do I do with that?" I said.

"I don't know," he said. "But I think we could learn a lot from you."

"We? I thought you were ..."

"Hey, I think I found one of your lenses—no, two."

"You're an angel from heaven," I said, sticking out my palms. "Thank you *so* much."

I popped the lenses into my mouth and then went to work at getting them into my eyes. When I blinked up at him, I nearly popped them both out again.

Looking back at me through Coke-bottle glasses was Mr. Head-in-the-History-Book.

He was giving me a slow smile. "Bummer, huh?" he said.

"What do you mean?" I stammered.

"I probably look better when you don't have your contacts in." But there was no sign that he was stung as he turned toward the kitchen and said, "All the pizza's going to be gone. They're animals."

"You're obviously not," I said quickly. Suddenly the last thing I wanted him to do was leave the room. "I mean, I know this sounds nerdy, but …"

"Nerdy?" he asked.

I unfolded from the floor and walked over to him. "Do you think you could give me some language lessons," I asked. "I mean, like, does anybody say 'Psych!' anymore?"

"Not unless they want to get hooted out of the room," he said.

He grinned at me. I looked into his glasses and saw myself. I was actually starting to smile back.

Don't Mess With the Creative Genius

S o what's this we're copying?" Shane said. *"La Granola?*
Sounds like something my mom sprinkles on her yogurt."

"I don't know. I can never pronounce all that French stuff,"
Brandi said. "I keep blinking my eyes to get it into focus. It
always looks fuzzy to me."

Matt blinked, too. "Oh. I thought it was just me."

I couldn't stand it any longer. The pencil I was using to cartoon in Claude Monet's painting on the wall went behind my
ear, and I glared at the three of them.

"It's *La Grenouillere*," I said. "This painting was the beginning of an innovative, avant-garde era in art." I looked straight
at Brandi. "And it isn't fuzzy. It's Monet's view of the world.
That's what impressionism is."

I left out: *Which you would know if you had been listening to
Ms. Walden's lecture.* I didn't want to give Ms. Walden credit for
actually knowing something. After all, she was just a substitute.

How much could a sub really know about art? Weren't they
sort of "general educators," filling in at the last minute on
anything? The thought of her talking about my beloved art

history—and the sight of these three artless wonders staring blankly from me to the wall to the art book on the floor—made me grab my pencil from behind my ear and go savagely back to work.

This project could have been so cool, I thought. The class was doing a mural of famous paintings on the walls in the hallway of the Fine Arts wing, and each small group had been assigned a work to copy. I thought I'd have to scratch and claw to get Monet, but the rest of the class had merely sat there with glazed eyes while Ms. Walden finally quit asking for preferences and just assigned people.

It would all have been different if Miss Delaquadri—the *real* teacher—had been there. She'd had to have major surgery just before school started, so we were stuck with Ms. Walden for eight weeks. I'd been looking forward to studying under Miss Delaquadri since I'd been in the fifth grade. Then I finally got to be a freshman in high school and this hippie chick waltzed in with her tie-dyed skirts and her combat boots and told us *she* was going to help us fall in love with my beloved Monet and Renoir and Cezanne. Miss Delaquadri could have inspired even bozos like Shane and Brandi, but Ms. Walden was obviously clueless.

I sniffed and went back to work. Who could believe she was sincere about anything? She had the nerve to wear a cross—a big ceramic job all painted up. Anybody could see she wasn't a Christian. After all, *Christians* weren't supposed to be concerned about wearing the latest fashions. Yet here she was, all decked out like something from *Seventeen* magazine. I hated it when people wore crosses because it was "cool" or because it was supposed to be art. To me, it was a privilege that should have been reserved for those of us who really loved the Lord.

"How do you know so much about this stuff, Cherise?" Brandi said.

I turned around and howled. She was standing there with a palette full of paint, and she was about to go after Monet's incredible background of trees with a paintbrush.

"What are you doing?" I demanded. "We aren't ready to paint yet. We haven't even finished cartooning!"

"What cartoon?" Shane said. He squinted his eyes at the painting as if he was looking for Bugs Bunny.

Brandi snickered. "Don't get her started, geek," she said.

"Geek?" Shane said. "Who're you calling a geek?"

"You," she said to him, and to my horror, she stuck her paintbrush into the green and flicked it at him.

His face spattered with pea soup-colored dots, Shane grabbed for the other paintbrush and sent blue-gray over Brandi's shoulder and onto my carefully cartooned rowboat.

"Oops," Matt said, slinking behind Shane.

At least he had the guts to admit somebody had done something unforgivable. Brandi and Shane just spewed laughter.

"I *hate* working with you guys!" I cried, snatching the palette from Brandi and stomping into the art room just as the bell rang.

Behind me I heard Shane say, "Well, *excuse* me!"

I slammed my books and stuff into my backpack so hard as I stormed out that I knocked a bunch of the sequins and puffy paint off the side of it. I made the repairs that night in my bedroom/studio while I discussed the situation with God.

"Everything about that art class is a disappointment," I told Him. "It isn't just Ms. Walden, although she's the worst part. I thought when I got to high school the art students would be *serious* about their work. But these upperclassmen don't revere art the way I do." The thought of Ms. Walden trying to stop them wasn't even a possibility.

"So, what do I do about it, God?" I said. "They're ruining something that's a gift from You."

I shoved a pile of *Smithsonian* magazines aside and pulled out my biggest volume on the impressionists. I fell asleep memorizing the second rowboat in *La Grenouillere.*

I woke up before the alarm with an idea. Whenever that happens, I always assume it's from God, so I stumbled out of bed in the dark, threw on a T-shirt and jeans, and tossed my backpack over my shoulder.

The only person in the school building at that hour was the janitor, and he strode over to me with his keys swinging importantly from his belt as if he were going to chew me out.

I didn't stop cartooning as I said, "Just trying to get caught up. It's a class project."

"Thought you was doin' graffiti," he said through the toothpick he was munching. "You're pretty good."

I sniffed to myself as he ambled away. It was pretty bad when the only person who appreciated your talent was a toothpick-chewing maintenance man.

I got a lot done before kids began arriving. At least, I *think* I did. I was oblivious to them. When that happens, I like to think God has taken over and I'm just holding the pencil. Ms. Walden probably said my name three times before I finally heard her.

"What's up, Cherise?" she said when I pried my eyes away from *La Grenouillere.*

I shrugged. "I just thought I'd come in and do some extra work. My group doesn't get much done during class."

Her eyebrows went up and I turned back to the wall.

"Do they know you're doing this?" she said.

"No."

"Don't you think you should have consulted them?"

"No!" I said sharply, then looked down at my nonexistent fingernails. "I don't think they'll care that much. They probably won't even notice."

Besides, I wanted to add, *this idea came from God, which, in spite of that cross you have hanging around your neck, you wouldn't know anything about.*

"You might be surprised," she said softly.

My heart pounded a strange beat as I watched her walk back into the art room. For a minute, I thought crazily that she'd read my mind.

When I rounded the corner near the art room before third period, Brandi, Shane, and Matt were standing in the hall in front of the now completely cartooned reproduction of *La Grenouillere.* Something about the way Brandi had her arms crossed over her chest and the way Shane dropped his books to the floor made me stop at the corner and listen.

"Did Cherise come in and do this?" Shane said.

"Who else?" Brandi said. "Unless Renoir showed up during the night."

"Who's Renoir?" Matt mumbled.

"What is *with* that chick?" Shane said.

"She's a freshman," Matt said.

But Brandi shook her mane of perfectly cascading curls. "No—freshmen are usually a pain, but not all of them are geeks."

Matt snickered and nodded. "Yeah—not all of them decorate their backpacks with puffy paint."

"It isn't just that, though." Brandi pointed a pearl-pink nail at the wall. "Look at this; She must have gotten here at 4 A.M. This was supposed to be *our* work, too."

"She's a freshmen fanatic," Shane said. He put his hand to the small of his back and leaned back to inspect the wall. "This painting was the beginning of an innovative, avant-garde era in art," he said in a shrill voice. "It's Monet's view of the world." He stood on his toes and loomed over Brandi's head. "That's what impressionism *is*, Stupid!"

Brandi giggled and smacked his face with a playful hand.

"Hey, I'm a creative genius!" Shane cried in the same shrill voice.

"Creative geek," Brandi said. "Come on. We have to talk to Ms. Walden."

"Whatever. Just don't mess with me," Shane said.

As they trailed into the room, I plastered myself against the wall so that the only thing moving was my heart—pounding that strange beat. Just as Shane reached the doorway behind the other two, he turned his head and saw me. Our eyes locked, and I could see every word he'd just spouted racing through his mind. He whipped around and lurched into the room, but I could still picture him with his hand in the small of his back, mocking me in a high-pitched voice.

Somehow I got to the nurse's office, convinced her I was coming down with the flu, and flopped onto a cot before I started to cry. Somewhere in the midst of my sobbing, I fell asleep. It was Ms. Walden who woke me up.

"It took me all period to find you," she said. "Brandi told me what happened." She smiled sadly at me. "We artists are often the only ones who understand each other. Maybe we can talk, huh?"

I shook my head. "I don't think we have that much in common."

There was silence in the clinic before she put her hand on my arm. "Maybe you don't respect me much as an artist or a teacher," she said, "but I ask you to respect me as a Christian."

I could feel my mouth dropping open as she said, "Let's talk, Christian to Christian."

I looked everywhere but at her, and she just waited. "I believe God gave me a gift," I said finally. "I'm just trying to use it, but they don't seem to care about anything except being popular and making fun of me. I was just trying to share my gift with them!"

"Share?" she said. "Or shove?"

"Shove?"

"You can't push your gift down people's throats like it's the only one God ever offered anyone, Cherise," she said. "Brandi and Shane and Matt aren't losers. They were wrong to make fun of you, but they have gifts, too. God's generous."

"Please let me do a project by myself!" I blurted out.

But she shook her curly head, and the cross swung sadly on its ribbon.

My mother didn't buy my attack of the flu the next morning, but I'd never felt sicker as I crept into the art room and tried to slip invisibly to our table. Right where I was about to drop my backpack sat a white envelope with "Cherise" written on it … in puffy paint.

Mystified, I picked it up and peeked inside.

There were three gloomy-looking, cartoonlike faces painted on the card. Below them, the words "We're sorry we're geeks" were scrawled in every color on the palette. I squinted to read the last line, printed in tiny purple letters.

"Forgive us?" it said.

I looked up. All three of them were huddled at the paint cabinet, watching. Brandi led the way toward me.

"Maybe it's not art—" she started to say.

"Looks like the Expressionistic period," I said.

They stared at me for a second, and then the smiles started melting across their faces.

"Do you, like, have a subscription to *Art Weekly* or something?" Shane asked.

"*Smithsonian,*" I said.

"See, that's the thing," Brandi said, tossing her mane. "Seriously, we're in awe that you're so smart and talented and everything. But when you start acting superior, we get ticked off and start being—"

"Geeks," Shane finished for her.

I looked at them all, their eyes so clear with honesty, and I could hear a thought—probably coming from God. *That's their gift, of course. They can be open with people. They never have to hide in studios and behind art books.*

"You aren't geeks," I said. "I came on pretty strong."

"Then will you still work with us?" Brandi said. "We could be good together."

I took a huge breath. "No more paint flicking?"

"Hey, that's cool with me," Shane said.

But there was one more thing I had to do, and while they finished mixing the colors, I sidled up to Ms. Walden's desk.

"Thanks for ... thanks for talking to me and stuff," I said.

She looked up from the copy of *Smithsonian* she was studying and smiled. Her paint-stained fingers went to the cross. "I don't think I really did much," she said, and then she pointed upward. "Thank the Creative Genius."

Later on, after we all painted in the rowboats, I did.

London Fog

think I want to become a fashion designer," I told Todd that afternoon at Candlewick Mall.

He leaned across the McDonald's table, shaking his head. "No, Jenna," he said. "I already know the job you're headed for. You're going to be a professional *shopper*."

I smacked at him with a napkin. "Todd!"

"I'm serious. You can't pass a shoe store."

"Stop it. I'm feeding you, aren't I?"

"Forget getting you by a jewelry counter without it costing forty, fifty bucks." He grinned. "You have the experience—the motivation. Why not make it a career?"

"You're being mean!" I said. But I smiled and dug into the Macy's bag by my foot. "If you don't knock it off, I won't give you the 'prise I got you today."

"Jen—you didn't buy me something again?"

"Of course I did. When you weren't looking."

Todd started to go into his embarrassed voice, but I pulled the hat out of the bag and plopped it on his head.

It was a great hat—and Todd loved hats—and I had the money to buy it for him.

"I love it!" I said. "You look like the Cat in the Hat!"

"You have to stop doing this."

"Why?" I asked. "My dad gives me a great allowance, and I can't spend it *all* on shoes. Besides, didn't you totally fall in love with it when you first saw it?"

Todd took it off and grinned at it. "Yeah, I did. Look at this, Jen, it's reversible."

"Squish it over this way. See how fun?"

Todd popped it back on and then cocked his head at me. "Even my mother says you spend too much on stuff for me."

"She'll change her mind when she sees what I got for *her*," I said. I pawed through the bag again. "Do you think she'll like this? I thought it would be neat for her desk."

Todd opened the box I produced and lightly touched the bisque figure of a little boy Jesus hugging a lamb.

"It isn't her birthday yet," he said.

"Why does it have to be? I love your mom. She's been really cool to me." I didn't add that on her salary as a church secretary and Todd's dad's as a computer something-or-other, she couldn't afford to treat herself to little luxuries.

"Want me to take it home to her?" he said.

"No, I thought I'd drop by the church." I pulled a notebook out of my purse. "Give me some directions, OK?"

Todd took the notebook from me and smelled it. "Jenna! This is real leather!"

"So?"

"Let me see your pen. Is it solid silver?"

"Todd, stop! You make me sound like Ivana Trump or something."

"What you couldn't do with *her* expense account."

He was teasing. I know he was.

But I still had a funny feeling when I hugged him good-bye in the mall parking lot and headed my dad's Mustang for the downtown church where his mother worked.

It really seemed to bother him that I had money—and I didn't get that. Yeah, my dad was an attorney, and yeah, my mom was an advertising executive, and yeah, we lived in Candlewick Hills. But I wasn't a snob. I was president of my church youth group. I was always heading up food drives and organizing walk-a-thons and starve-a-thons and read-a-thons for the hungry.

Besides, I was generous with what I had. For every new outfit I bought, somebody else always got a present too. And right now I was going to enjoy giving Mrs. Nielsen hers.

Since Todd and I had gotten to be friends, his mom had made me enough tuna casseroles and chocolate chip cookies to feed a small family for a month. I was always there for dinner or Saturday lunches or midnight snacks after basketball games, and she treated me like I was a member of the family. She was going to love the bisque.

I'd never been to the church where she worked. We went to a big, new one out in Candlewick. I finally found it on a side street facing the river, in a neighborhood I'd have never stumbled over myself. There were funny old hotels and thrift stores, and at one storefront a line of men stood outside waiting with their hands in their pockets.

But the church was actually beautiful, even through the spring rain that had started to dot the windshield. It was a huge, gray stone building at the top of a magnificent set of steps, and on the side that I could see as I parked the Mustang there was a long succession of stained glass windows that shimmered in the rain.

Trees surrounded the church, and some of them shed wet blossoms on me as I hurried toward the office building in the back. It was weird—I suddenly felt like I wanted to hurry, like there were eyes watching me that I needed to get away from.

Inside the glass doors, I took out my notebook and studied Todd's diagram. I was dully aware of a woman's harsh voice in the background. It got louder as I brushed the raindrops off my London Fog jacket and headed for the third door on the left.

"I about got it together now," the harsh voice said. "They want seven hunert down. Seven hunert!"

"I know how hard you've worked to put that much money aside," I heard Todd's mother say.

"It's them tips does it. Anyways, I could get out of the shelter and into the apartment *this* week, but I do that and the kid don't eat."

I saw "the kid" before I saw her. He had the biggest eyes I'd ever seen. Or maybe they just looked big because his face was so small and white.

"We just don't have any money left in the emergency till right now, Jessie," Mrs. Nielsen said.

"You know I ain't askin' for no handout, Joy," the woman said.

"No, you never have. But that doesn't mean we can't help out. If you didn't have to buy groceries this week—"

"I could get out of that shelter. I don't like the way them guys talk to the kid, y'know?"

Mrs. Nielsen nodded sympathetically and turned toward her

phone. That's when she spotted me and broke into a smile.

"Hi, Jenna! What a lovely surprise! Can you wait for a minute while I make a call?"

"Sure," I said. But I found myself gripping my purse and staring stiffly halfway between her and the floor. It was almost like she was going to leave me in the room with the woman with the voice like an Army sergeant, and it was suddenly scary.

"Carolyn, hi!" Mrs. Nielsen said into the phone. "Listen, we're finally going to see Jessie and little Taylor move into their own place, and I'm looking for a bag or two of groceries to get them started—"

The little boy whined, and I glanced over to see him raising his arms, asking to be picked up. His mother—Jessie—was looking at me. Really looking at me. Examining the label on my London Fog through the fabric from four feet away. I looked uncomfortably back at the floor. I couldn't tell you exactly what I felt. It was like I was over—well, over-something.

"All right, Jessie!" Mrs. Nielsen said. "Carolyn Cruz will be dropping off a couple of bags of goodies for you and the little guy tomorrow. Why don't you go pay that landlord the deposit and sign those papers?"

"You been good to me an' him," Jessie said. Even in gratitude, her voice was like a handful of gravel.

"You're easy to be good to," Mrs. Nielsen said.

I didn't agree. In fact, as soon as Jessie and little Taylor were gone, I said, "Do you get people like that in here all the time?"

"I do more social work than I do typing," Mrs. Nielsen said.

I hugged myself inside my coat. "How can you deal with that?"

When Mrs. Nielsen arched her eyebrows at me, I knew the question hadn't come out quite the way I'd wanted it to. Something flickered through her eyes.

I think that something was disappointment.

She liked the bisque figure. But giving it to her wasn't as much fun as I'd imagined it would be. It even looked ... over-something on her desk.

But when she asked me if I was coming over that night to study with Todd, my mood lifted a little. I didn't want her disappointed in me.

I was going over it all, the fuzziness of not knowing exactly what I was feeling, as I headed back out into the rain toward the car. Two figures were huddled near the Mustang's bumper. I think I'd have yelled at them if I hadn't noticed that I'd parked right next to a bus stop—and that the two wet figures were Jessie and Taylor.

For some reason still unknown to me, I didn't want them to see me. Naturally they did, the minute I unlocked the door and turned off the alarm.

I turned abruptly and thrust myself into the car, slamming the door on my coat. Grimacing, I opened the door to pull it in, shoulders hunched against—I don't know what. Did I expect her to snatch my purse? Pull out my tape deck? Make off with the leather notebook?

What I didn't expect was the gravelly voice calling to me through the rain. I leaned out and said, "What?"

"Take *care* of that coat now," she said. "The more it costs, the drier you are."

I slammed the door and with shaking fingers turned the key.

She watched as the power locks clicked.

I wondered as I pulled out hurriedly if I splashed her. She wasn't wearing a coat.

I wanted to tell Todd's mother how it all felt that night, but all I could put together in my mind was "over." I felt over-something. What? Overwhelmed? Overeducated?

Naturally, because I couldn't give it a name, I said something charming when she brought us hot chocolate, like, "I ran into your friend Jessie at my car."

Todd looked up from *Our American Heritage* and said, "Who's Jessie?"

"Todd," Mrs. Nielsen said, "this hot chocolate needs some marshmallows. Go get some, would you?"

"I ate the last ones this morning. Who's Jessie?"

"Looks like a trip to the 7-Eleven to me," she said.

"Take the Mustang," I said, tossing him the keys. Even that felt wrong. I slumped miserably while Todd finished bantering with his mother and went out the front door in his Cat-in-the-Hat hat.

"Did Jessie say something ugly to you?" she asked.

"Not exactly," I said. "I mean, her voice alone—"

"Is enough to scare the guys on death row," Mrs. Nielsen said drily. "Jessie's been through a lot. She's definitely a hard woman. But she's trying to make an honest life for herself and Taylor. What did she say, Jenna?"

"She made fun of my coat. She said the more it costs, the drier it will keep me, or something. I mean, I don't get it."

Mrs. Nielsen put her hand on my sleeve, like she was afraid I was going to bolt out of my seat on her next words.

"Shirt from Abercrombie, Jenna?" she said.

"Yeah."

"Calvin Klein jeans?"

"Uh-huh."

She gave my arm a squeeze. "When a person is struggling just to survive, it's easier for them to see what's really important. How much icing is on the cupcake means nothing to her when she doesn't even have bread."

After she said that, I felt more over-something than ever.

"Makes sense to me," Mrs. Nielsen said.

It didn't to me, not until the next day after school when I cruised the Mustang downtown to the church. It wasn't raining, and the ground was covered with manna-like tufts of cherry blossoms. I parked near the bus stop and with my London Fog over my arm got out to walk through them. I hadn't done that since I was a little kid, when I'd pretended they were magic gifts from the angels or something.

But my mind was now on finding Jessie. Taylor's whine led me to her, and I crossed the street to the river. Taylor, surrounded by muttering ducks, was doing the I'm-about-to-throw-a-tantrum stomp. Jessie was holding the remains of a sandwich out toward him.

"You ain't feeding this to no animals, Taylor. *You* eat it."

Taylor's voice wound up, while her gravel one wound down.

"Ducks!" he howled.

"You eat it!" she growled.

The crowd of mallards waited, grumbling impatiently.

I dug into my purse. Under the leather notebook was a bag

of pretzels. It came with the sandwich at Port of Subs, and I had been saving it to pacify Todd next time we went shopping.

Almost holding my breath, I walked toward them.

"Want to feed these to the ducks?" I said.

Jessie's head snapped around, and for an awful moment I thought she was going to throw *me* to the ducks. But Taylor happily snatched the bag of pretzels from my hand and dumped them on the ground. He chortled up and down the scale as the ducks inhaled them.

And Jessie laughed. She actually laughed. It sounded like gravel being dumped into a bathtub, but it was a laugh.

I noticed then that she and Taylor were on an almost transparent blanket on the ground, having a picnic. It was barely the first week of spring—the air was still damp and shivery—but the sandwiches were there, and a few apples, and a carrot they were sharing. Carolyn's groceries.

"I brought you something," I said.

Jessie looked at me sharply. "Me?"

"Yeah, I thought—"

"I don't take nothing unless it's got a decent label," she said. The gravel hit the bathtub again.

"It does," I said stupidly, and I held out my London Fog.

Jessie stared at it, then at me, then back at the coat.

"Please—it's yours," I said. I felt that over-something feeling again, and I just wanted her to take the coat so I could get out of there.

"Sure," she said, plucking it from my hand. "I mean, you probably got a dozen more at home, right?"

Her sarcasm was like a wad of cardboard in my throat as I hurried back to the car, but I swallowed it. It was OK, actually, because now I knew what I'd been feeling.

Over-something.

Overdone.

Overdressed.

Overfed.

Under-human.

I didn't get into the Mustang after all. Instead, I took off down the sidewalk and stepped through the pink tufts of angel magic. I seemed to feel lighter without the coat.

I *Would* Just Be Myself—If I Knew Who I Was!

Bloopers

Cameron—ready with the tape?"

"Yeah."

"Are you sure my makeup looks OK in this light, Marcie?"

"Uh-huh."

"Have you got the camera focused right this time? Brice? Brice!"

"What?"

"Is the camera ready?"

My brother lowered the camcorder from his eyes and narrowed them at me. "Yes, it's ready," he said in an impatient voice. "It's *been* ready for the past fifteen minutes."

"Lighten up," Emily said. She took off the visor I was making her wear—after all, she *was* the director—and smeared the sweat off her forehead. The lights Cameron had put up for me made my living room feel like a steam bath. I motioned to Marcie for more powder.

"Can't you see she's freaking out?" Emily said to Brice. "Just humor her."

"I'm not freaking *out!*" I said.

"Then how do we account for the veins bulging out of the sides of your head?" Brice said.

There was a round of snickers—except from Cameron, who was tapping his fingers on the top of the piano.

"Could we hurry this up?" he said. "I've got a tech rehearsal at six."

"I know," I said, glaring at the rest of them. "That's why I picked you—because you're a professional."

Brice snorted. "He's in the high school theatre tech pool! You really are getting delusions of grandeur over this whole thing, Andrea."

"I am not," I said stubbornly. "You know how much this means to me. I just want it to be perfect."

"It'll be fabulous," Emily said. "But only if we actually *finish* it. Can we start the shoot?"

I gave them all one last warning stare before I turned to the piano and placed my hands in perfect bear claws on the keys. "All right," I whispered. "I'm ready."

Cameron pushed the button on the tape player, and I heard my own voice, sounding crystalline and measured, explaining that I practiced Christian music at least an hour a day. It really did sound good, the little speech I'd recorded. It should have. I had only done it about sixteen times.

At precisely the right moment, I started to play, and my voice faded out under the music. Perfect. It was all perfect. Until I hit the last chord and was suddenly in some weird-sounding key. I crossed my eyes and moaned.

"Aw, man. You were doing so great!" Emily said.

Brice snickered again. "I got those crossed eyes right on film. Next shot!"

"No, Brice!" I said. "We have to do it over."

"Du-uh," he said. He rolled his eyes at Emily, who rolled hers at Marcie, who—well, you get the idea. Then we went back to the beginning and started over.

This time it was perfect. Well, almost perfect. I would have loved to redo the phrasing on that one section, but I was afraid the whole crew would mutiny. They'd already reminded me three times that we'd been at it since 9 A.M.—right after my makeover at Merle Norman—taking shots at the Sunday school nursery where I took care of the babies, then screaming over to the mission in time for them to get me on film serving lunch to the homeless, and then setting everything up here at my house to get some footage of me praying in my sacred space, reciting Galatians while cleaning the toilets, and now, the grand finale, honing my God-given talents at the piano.

Now they reminded me that it was time for me to pay up.

"You promised us a six-foot sub," Brice said as he sniffed the air. "I don't smell it."

"Can't you think of anything besides your stomach?" I said. "We'll eat *after* we look at what we've got."

I made a grab for the camera, but Brice snatched it out of my reach, and the room erupted in protests of, "No way! We eat now or the tape goes into the garbage disposal!" I knew they would mutiny.

I yelled for Mom, and she and my dad came in with a submarine sandwich the size of the *Titanic.* Cameron, Marcie, and Emily went after it like a flock of vultures. I went after Brice.

"Give me the tape," I said. "I'm afraid you'll spill something on it."

"Would you chill?" he said. "I'm not gonna let anything happen—oops!"

He pretended to fumble the tape and I gave him my best younger-sister glower, the one where my eyebrows go down to my upper lip.

"Very funny," I said. "Now hand it over."

"Look, I know you think *you're* Spielberg, but it has to be edited first."

"When will it be done?"

"Maybe tonight—if I don't starve to death first."

"You could go get started on it," I suggested. "I'll bring a piece of sandwich in to you."

"Andy," my father said, "give it a rest."

He gave me his best *father* glower, and I tried not to pout as I popped open a can of Diet Coke and sat restlessly on the floor beside Emily.

"Since when did you start drinking diet soda?" she asked.

"Since she found out the camera adds ten pounds," Marcie said.

Cameron blinked at me, tech-geek fashion. "You're kidding, right?"

"Look," I said. "I know you guys think I went a little overboard with this whole thing …"

"Overboard?"

"No way!"

"I think asking your mother to redo the living room for the photo shoot was perfectly reasonable."

"… but I just wanted to make a good impression on the acceptance committee," I finished.

"They're going to think you're incredible," Emily said. She gave my leg one of those best-friend punches. "I know we've all gotten a little sick of you stressing out over this, but you really have put a lot of work into it. I don't see how they *couldn't* take you."

I hugged my knees to my chest. "I still wish you'd let me ask Dr. James Dobson for a recommendation."

"You've met the man once," Dad said.

"And like he would really remember you," Brice said as he reached for another hunk of sandwich. *"These* people are going to remember you. Who else would videotape herself saying Bible verses with her head in the commode?"

"What?" Dad asked.

"Do you really think I'll stand out?" I said. "This thing is so competitive …"

"We've heard this eighty times," Emily said. She went into her I-have-this-memorized voice. "World Changers takes only fifty people for this program, and kids from all over the country will be applying, and the application form and the letters of reference and the essay and the videotape all have to be perfect or they'll think you're pond scum and not even consider you for New Mexico."

"And at this point," Brice said, "I would gladly ship you off there myself. You've about driven me crazy with this thing."

I reminded him that that would be a putt, not a drive, and he pounded me with a pillow. Then, since I was down already, Emily and Marcie started tickling me, and then Cameron flipped on the Newsboys just to add a little background noise, and for a while I forgot about World Changers. You know, for about ten minutes.

Really, it wasn't until they'd all gone home and Brice had

promised me that he was going straight to his room to start editing my video and would call me the minute it was done—it wasn't until then, when I was in my room, on my bed, staring at the ceiling, that I went back to obsessing.

There was no other word for it. Ever since I'd picked up the brochure at church and read about how this camp being held in New Mexico was going to help committed Christian teens seriously deepen their faith and understand God's will for them, I hadn't been able to think about anything else. And once the application packet had arrived, I'd gone into serious overload and had taken everybody with me.

Mom spent hours typing my application for me, and I begged my father ad nauseam to let me ask Dr. Dobson for a recommendation. I had to settle for our pastor and my Bible study teacher, who I'd heard had gotten straight *A*s in Bible college.

The two-page essay nearly maxed everybody out. My father told me that if I didn't stop waking him up in the middle of the night to ask how to spell words, he was either going to chain me to a dictionary or put the kibosh on the whole project. So I chained my*self* to a dictionary and put out an essay my English teacher said was worth an *A*-plus. Still, I asked her, "But do you think *Jesus* would give it an *A*-plus?"

I guess it did get a little bit out of control, because by the time we got to making the videotape, people were saying no to me right and left. Marcie, who was in the scene with me at school where we were doing peer mediation, refused to get a makeover, Mom wouldn't get new drapes for the living room, and I had to bribe Brice to look up the Scripture quotations I wanted to use in five different translations so I'd get the ones that sounded the very best. I'd have done it myself, but I was really busy doing all my subtitles in calligraphy for the video.

The thing is, though, I *had* to do it. Seriously. I didn't just *want* to go to New Mexico. I was *dying* to go. I was salivating. I was clawing at the carpets. I wanted it *bad*.

As I lay on my bed that night with all the preparations behind me and the whole thing now in somebody else's hands, I totally started to cry. Tears were running out the sides of my eyes, into my ears, and I could barely see the ceiling.

"I want this so much, God," I whispered, "I know it has to be coming from You. Please guide the people who are going to make this decision. Please let them know that You want me there. I've done everything I can do. I pray I've done right."

There was a tap on the door, and I sat up and slapped at the tears.

"Yeah?" I said.

Brice poked his head in and said, "You wanna see the tape?"

As we sat in his room and watched my video even my brother didn't make any sarcastic remarks. I think we were both amazed at the girl who appeared on the screen, looking like every mother's dream of a perfect Christian daughter. To tell you the truth, I barely recognized her.

"Wow," I said when Brice snapped off the TV.

"Yeah," he said. And then he looked at me sideways. "If you tell anybody I said this, I'll deny it. But if they don't accept you, they won't accept anybody."

The packet went out the next day. The letter came an agonizing two weeks later. If my family and friends thought I'd driven them crazy before, they hadn't seen anything.

I had Emily and Marcie saying "Shut *up!*" in unison every time I brought it up. But when I called to tell them the letter had arrived and I didn't want to open it until everybody was there, they were at my house in record time. Mom baked brownies, and even Dad said we ought to have sparkling cider for the occasion. He was just popping it open when I couldn't stand it any longer and tore into the envelope.

"Drum roll," Emily said, still playing the director.

Cameron hammered one out on the coffee table, and Marcie bounced up and down like she had to go to the bathroom.

"Quiet!" Dad commanded, although no one was saying anything.

They all leaned in as my eyes took in the first paragraph. I wanted to savor the words myself before I read it out loud.

Dear Andrea:

Thank you for your application to the World Changers camp in New Mexico. Although your packet was impressive and you are obviously a fine Christian young person, we are unable to invite you to join us this summer …

I stopped reading. There was an uneasy silence in the room.

"What does it say, Honey?" Mom asked.

"They don't want me," I said. My trembly little voice sounded nothing like the confident young woman on the video.

"May I see it?" Mom asked.

I handed it to her numbly as I felt Emily's arm go around my shoulder, and I saw through a blur that Marcie was trying to hand me a Diet Coke. I closed my eyes and let the tears come.

"It says here they had over five hundred applicants," Mom said.

"What do you want to bet you were number fifty-one on the list?" Dad said.

If that was meant to make me feel better, it might as well have been a dose of arsenic. I buried my face in my knees, and that's where I still was when everybody finally got up and left, leaving the sparkling cider and the brownies untouched.

I would have stayed that way, too, if Mom hadn't made me go to school the next day and Dad hadn't made me come to the dinner table and Brice hadn't made me tell him to get out of my face when he told me to "cheer up." Basically, I went through the motions of my usual life, but I felt like a crushed version of my former self.

When I finally got to lock myself in my room at night, I'd lie on my back again and cry to God. "I let You down! I know You wanted me to do this, and I blew it!"

Marcie and Emily tried to console me, but I was a lost cause. They took me to the mall, put a stuffed animal in my locker, and told me they were praying for me. Even Cameron tried, as best a tech geek knows how. He offered to let me sit in the booth with him during a dress rehearsal for the school play. I declined.

On Friday of the second week of mourning, I noticed them starting to get peeved with me.

"Andy, could you at least smile?" Emily said at lunch.

"What for?" I said. "I feel like a total failure."

"Get a grip already! Do you think you're the only person who's ever been disappointed?" Marcie asked. "Did I carry on like this when I didn't make cheerleader?"

I gave her a blank look. She had no idea. It wasn't the disappointment at not making it. It was the horrible, sinking feeling that I'd let God down somehow, that He'd given me an opportunity and I just hadn't been good enough.

But that night, as I lay on my bed again, begging the ceiling to forgive me, the door to my bedroom burst open, and there they all were: Brice, Cameron, Emily, and Marcie. Cameron was carrying a rope, and Brice made a big deal out of handing Marcie a bandanna before he came over to the bed and picked me up. I threw my head back to scream, and that was when Marcie tied the bandanna around my mouth and Emily led the way to the family room.

"Muffa-muffa-muffa!" I said.

"Oh, you want to be tied to the chair?" Brice asked.

He nodded to Cameron, who executed some kind of fancy knot, and I was confined to the La-Z-Boy. "Glower" doesn't even come close to describing the look I gave them.

"Run the tape," Emily said.

Brice pointed the remote and suddenly the TV lit up with a picture of me playing the piano with perfect poise, making a big old sour mistake, and crossing my eyes right into the camera. Brice snorted, and Marcie started to giggle. I kicked against the rope.

Then there was me at the mission, putting whipped cream onto sundaes, getting a dab on the tip of my nose, and licking it off with my tongue. Even Cameron got a guffaw out of that one.

And then there was me, being tickled on the floor by Emily and Marcie, and then doing some kind of lame can-can dance with them, and then blowing raspberries on a baby's tummy and making him giggle, and then glaring at the camera and saying, "Brice, don't use that!"

It didn't take a rocket scientist to figure out that these were all the outtakes from my perfect video. What it did take me some time to realize was that I really liked the girl I was seeing. She might have squealed like a delighted piglet and made a complete fool out of herself every other minute, but she seemed so real to me.

And she was nothing like the girl on the video I'd mailed off to World Changers.

When it was over, I'd stopped kicking and making muffa-muffa sounds under the gag. They took off the ropes and the bandanna in a strange kind of silence. It was like they were all suddenly uneasy, like the whole thing hadn't had quite the effect they'd planned on.

Leave it to Brice to speak for all of them.

"You know what?" he said, still staring at the blank screen. "I think they would have taken you if you'd sent this tape instead of the other one."

My first reaction was to hurl a pillow at him, and I did that. But everybody else was nodding. I looked at each one of them in turn.

"You don't really think that, do you?" I asked.

"Nah," Marcie said. She looked at Emily, "Do I?"

"Well, kind of," Emily said.

They both looked at Cameron, who, of course, shrugged. They all turned to Brice, but I was the one who spoke up.

"If they'd taken me because of the tape I sent," I said, "they would have been disappointed when I got there, because that was the me I polished up and put in just the right light."

"The lighting *was* good," Cameron muttered.

"But they wouldn't have taken me on the basis of this one either," I went on.

"Why not?" Marcie said. "I like this Andy better."

"What?" I said. "Messing up all the time and doing weird stuff?"

"And being real?" Emily said. "I liked you better in this one, too. It's like the best part of you is when you're making mistakes or something."

Brice chose that moment to throw the pillow back at me, but it didn't hit me any harder than the thought that slammed into my head at the same time.

"Whoa," I said.

"Get that rope ready," Brice said. "She just had a thought."

"No. I'm serious," I said. "Maybe the reason they didn't want me was because I looked *too* perfect, like I made it look like I didn't have anything left to learn."

"I never fix something that isn't broken," Cameron said.

We all blinked at him for a minute, like *we* were tech geeks.

And then we hunted up the brownies my mom had stuck in the freezer and put them in the microwave, and I dug in the fridge for a real Coke.

And we actually talked about something else that night besides my video and my application and my letters of reference. I didn't think about them again until I was in bed later. Just before I went to sleep, I made a promise to God.

"From now on, God," I whispered to the ceiling, "I'm going with the bloopers."

Confessions of a Fat Girl

Kristine—is that actually you?"

"Look at you, Kristine! I hardly recognized you!"

"You look incredible!"

I have to admit I stood there and basked in it for a minute. You don't spend a whole summer eating salads without Thousand Island and not glow in the result just a little.

Ashley wrapped her well-manicured fingers around my arm. "What made you do it? Did you just get tired of being fa—"

"Clothes are just more fun to buy in the petite department, right?" Desirée cut in.

Actually, it was neither. It had more to do with my body being a temple. But suddenly I wasn't sure about quoting St. Paul to two cheerleaders I'd admired from afar since sixth grade.

"How much weight did you *lose?*" Ashley squealed.

"About twenty pounds," I said. "I'm still working on it, though."

"Don't lose another ounce," Desirée said. "You look amazing." She bobbed her chin toward where the Tornadoes were taking the field. "And I'm not the only one who thinks so."

Ashley leaned in to shout conspiratorially over the roar of the crowd in the bleachers behind us.

"It was Gary who told me to—how did he put it, Des?—oh, yeah, 'Check out Kristine Westmore.' He said you must have dumped fifty pounds—"

"But what do guys know about weight?" Desirée cut in again. "The point is, you *have* to come to the party at Ashley's after the game. Then he can really check you out!"

They both tossed their hair. I couldn't help it. I tossed mine, too.

Ashley poked me. "So, will you come?"

"Where's your house?" I asked.

"Oh, that's right—you've never hung with us before." Ashley gave my new figure one more approving once-over with her eyes. "You know Smokey Vista?"

Everyone knew Smokey Vista Drive. Driving a Porsche didn't get you as much clout as living on Smokey Vista.

"We've gotta go cheer," Desirée said. "But why don't we meet right here at the gate after the game? You can go with us."

That's when it hit me. I'd already heard those words earlier that afternoon—in more familiar voices. *"We'll meet you at the gate right after the game,"* Caroline, Mikey, and Jenny had said to me when we'd left Round Table Pizza that afternoon.

"You don't have a swimsuit with you, do you?" Ashley said.

"Like she carries one in her purse!" Desirée said.

Ashley tossed her hair again. "No problem. You can wear one of mine."

She went on to say that their pool was still warm for the first month of football games but I really didn't hear much of that.

Nor did I pay attention to any of the voices in my own head that were saying, *"We'll meet you at the gate right after the game."*

All I could think about was being able to fit into one of Ashley Barrett's swimsuits.

Yes.

* * * * *

I like to think I was looking for Mikey and Jen and Caroline *before* I ran into the three of them at the gate. But if I'm honest with myself I think I was actually peering into the crowd for Desirée and Ashley when Mikey blew his trumpet in my ear.

"The band geeks are here," Jen said. "Let the reveling begin!"

Caroline was already unbuttoning the collar of her uniform. "We'll get changed and then we can go to Round Table."

My mind was racing. These were my best friends, but how often did I get invited up to Smokey Vista Drive by the crowd that basically ran this school? Why had I eaten all that broccoli without butter—wasn't it so I could see what more there was to life?

"Actually, there's a party," I said.

Three pairs of eyebrows shot up under white-plumed shakers.

"What kind of party?"

"Where?"

"Who's giving it?"

"Yikes," I said. "What's with the inquisition? I was invited to Ashley Barrett's—"

"Oh, excuse me for living!"

"Did she ask to see your gold card?"

"Knock it off, you guys!" I said. "Ashley and Desirée invited me and—"

"Desirée, too?" Mikey said. He gave a sour fanfare on his trumpet.

Jen pushed her glasses up on her nose and peered at me. "I'm sure their invitation didn't include us, so if you're going to that party we'll see you later."

Caroline tugged at the uniform buttons that gaped open over her stomach.

"Why don't *you* come with me," I said to her.

"No thanks. I prefer to hang out with people a little higher on the food chain."

"Was I like this last year?" I said.

"Like what?"

"Putting down everybody who was different from us, being all bitter because some people have it better?"

"Last year you thought cheerleaders and football players and student council biggies were all a bunch of glory-seeking light-mongers. Now you're going to go party with them!"

"Don't you ever wonder if there's anything out there besides Round Table?"

Caroline thoughtfully licked the tiny dots of sweat off her upper lip. "Not if you're talking about the cheerleader brain trust. But if that's what you're looking for, knock yourself out."

* * * *

"You know what's, like, so weird?" Gary said.

I shook my head—and tugged self-consciously at the bottoms of Ashley's hot pink two-piece.

"Usually after a game, I'm, like, totally hyper. All I want to do is, like, tear something up, ya' know what I'm saying?"

I didn't, but I nodded anyway. What difference did it make? I was talking to the running back with the shoulders. He'd been only a number on a jersey to me until tonight—and I'd been nothing to him.

"But right now," he went on, "all I want to do is sit here and talk to you. That's, like, so weird."

He smiled at me for a minute and then took a long drag out of his Dr. Pepper can, never taking his eyes off of me as he drank. I looked down at the top of my unopened Diet Pepsi can and tried not to scream, "Yes! Yes! Yes!"

"So are you going to introduce me, or are you going to be a jerk and keep her all to yourself?"

We both looked up at Ryan Mifflin, whose blue eyes were zoned in on me like two laser beams. I didn't point out that we had been in the same math classes since seventh grade and that an introduction was probably entirely unnecessary. I just stared back at him—and then down at my Diet Pepsi.

"In your dreams," Gary said, but he got up and looked down at me. "You better still be here when I get back," he said. Then he wiggled an eyebrow and sauntered off.

Ryan sat down and stuck out his hand. "Ryan Mifflin," he said.

"I know," I said.

"No, see, actually, you don't." Ryan looked around and then leaned in. I adjusted the straps on the two-piece. "A lot of people think they 'know' me because I let them think they do. But you know what's weird?"

I shook my head and got the oddest sensation of déjà vu as Ryan told me how much he really just felt like talking to me.

Weird.

"You found one, then," Ashley said to me, nodding approvingly at the big T-shirt I'd just snagged from her dresser. She'd given me free reign when I'd told her I was cold. Actually, I just wasn't used to sitting around in something smaller than my underwear.

"You've got great legs," Desirée said. "Have you thought about trying out for cheerleader next year?"

"How about her?" Gary said. "Why don't you ask her to try out?"

We all followed his eyes to the glass doors that led from the house to the pool. Ryan was talking to a girl who had twenty pounds on anybody on the patio. I stifled a gasp.

"Who is that, anyway?" Ashley asked.

I didn't answer, but I knew. It was Caroline.

Ashley stood up. "I hate it when somebody crashes my party."

Gary grabbed her arm and jerked her back down. "Chill. Ryan's going to mess with her mind."

Ryan had backed Caroline against the house and had his hand up on the wall over her head. Her face was expressionless—and bright red.

"Heaven only knows what he's saying to her," Desirée said. "You ought to go stop him, Gary."

"No—check it out. He's got her goin' already."

"Why is he talking to a fat girl?" Ashley asked.

Desirée poked her. "That's so mean!"

"Well, she is. Look at that—her thighs are, like, twice as big as mine. That is so gross."

"Maybe she can't help it. Maybe she has a gland thing."

"Maybe she's just a pig," Gary said.

Ashley slapped him, but she laughed. Me? I just stood there, frozen, not saying a word to defend my best friend.

"What's he doing now?" Ashley said.

Caroline had slid out from under Ryan's arm and was backing away from him. Ryan bore down on her, moving her right toward the pool.

"Gary, stop him!" Desirée said.

"No way—this is *funny.*"

"Oh, no!" Ashley squealed with delight.

I watched in horror as Caroline stepped backward into the water. Cans were dropped on tables and Doritos left uneaten in mid-bite as everyone looked and howled and pointed. I finally came unfrozen and bolted for poolside. Ashley caught my arm.

"I wouldn't," she whispered.

And I didn't.

At least I didn't until Caroline had hauled herself out with her T-shirt stuck to her skin, outlining every bulge and dimple. She'd already gotten to the door—and Ashley had already yelled, "Don't go in the house without drying off first!"—when I finally shook off Ashley's hold and went to Caroline, snatching the towel from around Gary's neck on the way.

"Here," I said to her.

She took the towel from me and covered her face with it as we both walked through the house for the front door. Pool water dropped angrily on the marble floor.

"Do you get it now?" she said to me when we were outside. "These people are animals!"

"I'm sorry, Caroline—"

"Why should you be sorry? You're not one of them—" She peered out at me from under the towel. "Are you?"

Something clicked in me—something I'd almost forgotten until now.

"That's not why I lost weight," I said.

"Don't kid yourself, Kristine."

"No, I did it because of the temple thing."

"What temple thing?"

"How the Bible says your body's a temple of the Holy Spirit and you shouldn't abuse it. You know the verses, Caroline. You sit right there beside me in church."

"You're seriously telling me you did it—"

"For God," I said.

She shook her head. "And did you team up with the beautiful people 'for God'?"

"I'll admit it—I got caught up in all the attention and stuff. And besides, you and Jen and Mikey were being so cynical and bitter."

"Excuse me for being real," Caroline said. She jammed the towel down on a wicker chair and turned to go.

"Hey," I said. "Why did you decide to come anyway?"

She smiled caustically over her shoulder. "I thought you might need a friend," she said.

I was dressed and washing out Ashley's swimsuit when Desirée came in. I glanced at her in the mirror and kept rinsing.

"You're leaving, then?" she asked.

"This isn't my kind of party."

"She's a friend of yours, huh?"

"She? You mean Caroline? She *was* a friend—until I let *your* friends dump her into the pool."

"I'm really sorry that happened. You're a cool person, Kristine."

"And what if I gain twenty pounds back?" I said. I grabbed my purse and turned to go. She caught my hand softly.

"People sort of stick with people who are like them. We invited you over because now you look like us. But you're not— and that's what's cool."

I pulled my hand away and said, "Ashley's T-shirt's on her bed."

But as I went out the door, Desirée said stubbornly, "I'm going to call you."

As I sat on Ashley's front curb, waiting for my dad to come pick me up, I realized it was the first time that night I hadn't had somebody babbling in my ear. That's when my own voice started in.

Well, girl, it said, *why did you bother with all the diet soda and bread sticks?*

And then it clicked again, only louder this time. It really would be a bummer if the reason I'd lost weight was to get in with the "right" crowd. But all those days I passed up banana splits in favor of nonfat yogurt and swam laps when everyone else was tanning in lounge chairs—getting in with the right crowd hadn't been the reason.

I'd truly been thinking about Paul's thing about your body being a temple of God's Spirit inside of you that you needed to take care of.

And what had that gotten me?

Proof that Caroline was friend enough to venture into enemy territory to be sure I was all right.

A warning that guys with big shoulders are not necessarily to die for.

A mental poke that said my friends and I had judged people by appearances, too, and thought the resulting cynicism was "being real."

And the promise of a new friend.

The headlights of our Bronco appeared around the corner and I stood up. That was going to require some heavy praying. But first maybe Dad would drop me off at Round Table. There were some *old* friends there who needed to hear this.

Sophie's Choice

SCENE ONE

MRS. CHESTERFIELD: Sophie, I really hope you'll accept this role because, frankly, there isn't anyone else in the department right now who could even come *close* to portraying KATHIE the way you can.

SOPHIE: I don't know, Mrs. C. I have so *many* commitments …

MRS. C.:   Please, Sophie. The success of the show depends on you …

Actually, that wasn't *exactly* the way it happened. What really happened was that I went through the auditions like everyone else, chewing my nails up to the armpit the entire time. Then, the day the casting was posted, I waited until the crowd around the callboard splintered off, and I crept up to it as if the list would lash out and cut me to ribbons if my name weren't on it.

But not only was my name up there, it was at the top of the list, next to KATHIE.

KATHIE—the female lead. The character who made the audience cry into their programs, who took her last curtain call with the crowd screaming for more ...

Well, it was a good role, the kind I'd dreamed about since I did my first backyard Cinderella when I was five. The kind every girl in the department wanted, and that I'd never even had the guts to try out for until now.

"All *right*, Sophie!"

I turned around to a face full of freckles. It belonged to Eric Brolin, the Drama Club president.

"You got a plum your first time out," he said.

"Yeah." I shrugged and felt my face turning the color of watermelon. Why was it I could get up on stage and perform for a theatre full of people, but I could barely carry on a conversation with one other human being? "I don't know if I'll be able to pull this off," I said. "I mean—a girl in a girl's home, trying to get her life together—"

"Come on, your audition was awesome. You blew Tabby and all those other 'vets' off the stage."

"But I haven't even read the whole script yet."

Eric grinned a grin that folded his freckles into dashes. "You neophytes," he said. "When you've been around the theatre as long as I have, you learn how to get around these minor roadblocks."

He reached into his jacket and pulled out a little white book.

"The script?" I asked.

"It isn't my algebra book, sweetheart."

Tenderly, I took it from him like it was a sacred relic. It represented more than just my first big part. It meant I finally belonged somewhere in high school. Being a Christian—and trying to actually *live* what I believed—made it hard to fit in sometimes. I brushed my fingers across the cover. Maybe now I'd found a "home."

"Will you stop massaging it and go read it?" Eric said.

I smiled at him and stuffed it into my binder. "Thanks," I said.

There was a swish of jeans behind us, and we turned to look. You always looked when Tabatha Peters entered the area, I'd discovered. She didn't appear to see us as she sailed past, tossing her hair back as if it, like just about everything else in the world, annoyed her to no end.

"Uh-oh," Eric said out of a hole he formed at the side of his mouth.

"What?" I asked, out of a similar hole.

He was going to answer me when Tabatha pivoted around. Her eyes were wild. "Who's Sophie Crawford?" she demanded.

Eric smiled and pointed to me.

Tabatha seemed to find that hard to believe. She gaped for a second, and then whipped around to scrutinize the callboard again—as if maybe the names had rearranged themselves.

"See you at the cast meeting after school," Eric said to me, out of the hole. "But you'd better split now."

I did. As I turned the corner I heard Tabatha say, "Has she ever even *done* theatre before?"

SCENE TWO

MRS. CHESTERFIELD: How did you like the script, Sophie?

SOPHIE: It's a magnificent piece of writing, Mrs. C. I think I have some of the best dialogue in the play.

But that wasn't what happened, either. What really happened was that I raced through my geometry theorems first hour so I could read the script. Before the bottom of the first page I could see KATHIE—me—staring, angry and frightened, at her fellow "inmates," crying as she struggled to find answers, swearing at the—

Swearing.

I slapped the script onto my desk.

My character had to *swear*.

I hadn't been expecting iambic pentameter. KATHIE was a juvenile delinquent, after all. But I hadn't expected her to swear like a truck driver.

I hadn't expected Sophie to have to, either.

It was one of the ways I practiced my Christianity. I didn't drink. I respected my parents. And I didn't swear.

I picked up the script and stared at it again. Sophie didn't swear. But KATHIE did.

SCENE THREE

SOPHIE: Eric, have you read this whole script?

ERIC: Yeah, for the first time today. Can you believe the language in this thing? We're all upset about it. A bunch of us are going to protest to Mrs. Chesterfield.

SOPHIE: May I join you?

I don't even have to mention that that wasn't what happened that afternoon at the cast meeting when I told Eric I couldn't say some of the stuff in KATHIE's lines.

"Why not?" he asked.

"It's bad language. I don't talk like that."

He stared until his freckles flattened out. "It's no big deal. You open your mouth and your character says—"

"I can't do it," I said. "I've never talked like that and I never will."

"Then be prepared to give your role to Tabby," he said. "She's salivating for it already."

Tabby was sitting on the edge of the stage, alternating between glaring at the script and glaring at me. When our eyes met, hers went into narrow little points and she flipped her hair at me.

"Why does she hate me?" I said.

"Because you got what she wanted," Eric said. "She and about six other girls." He gave a hard little laugh. "If I were you, I'd become a little less of a religious fanatic for about six weeks."

I stared at my shoelaces during most of the time Mrs. Chesterfield talked about the rehearsal schedule and the professionalism she expected from us. But when she announced that tomorrow we'd do our first read-through my head snapped up.

"Out loud?" I asked.

There was a smattering of snickers.

"That was the idea," Mrs. Chesterfield said. "Unless you were planning to pantomime your role."

My face was burning by then, and I just clutched the script and shook my head.

Somebody, probably Tabatha, hissed through her teeth.

"All right," Mrs. Chesterfield said, "then have your lines highlighted by tomorrow and we'll get started."

"I *know* that Sophie person has never done theatre before," I heard Tabatha say. "This ought to be *very* interesting."

SCENE FOUR

MOM:	I'm calling the school. *No* child should be forced to use language like that on a high school stage.
SOPHIE:	Mother, it's all right. I'll just give my role to Tabatha.
MOM:	It's the principle of the thing, Sophie. The script will be changed by tomorrow afternoon.

Not!

My mother was waiting at the door to find out if I'd gotten a part. When I told her I'd been given *the* part, she headed straight for the kitchen to make celebration chocolate chip cookies. When I showed her what the character was required to say, she propped the wooden spoon in the cookie dough, and her eyes actually got tears in them.

"Why do they have to put you kids in that position?" she asked. And then she hugged me. "But God never said it was going to be easy to be a Christian."

I pulled back and looked at her. "Aren't you going to do something?" I asked.

She started to stir again. "I don't think I can start a club—Mothers Against Swearing."

"It isn't funny!"

"No, it isn't." She banged the spoon on the side of the bowl.

"So, what do I do?" I asked.

"Well, you have two options, as I see it. You can give up the role. Or you can say the lines."

"Say them! Wouldn't you hate that?"

"Yes."

"Then—"

"*You* have to decide, Honey."

"Mom, please!" I said. "Just tell me what you'd do—"

She put her head in the cabinet and groped for the cookie sheets. "Not fair," she said. "I'm not the one who has my heart set on being an actress. For you, it's the first of a thousand decisions like this you'll have to make. You might as well start now."

"You're not going to help me?"

"I'd ask God to help me, if I were you."

SCENE FIVE

SOPHIE: And so, Lord, that's my dilemma. What's the right answer?

Suddenly in SOPHIE's *room, a heavenly light seems to shimmer from the walls. At first she is frightened, until a soft voice comes from nowhere ...*

Right. I tossed and turned and prayed most of the night, and there was no heavenly light, no voice, soft or otherwise, and definitely no audible answer. I didn't even get a feeling of peace the way I usually do after I've prayed about something and the right decision takes shape. I was still just as confused after school the next day as I had been the night before.

One minute I'd imagine myself nobly giving up the role—and crying for the next six weeks. I loved the theatre.

Then I'd see myself going ahead with the role—and feeling like my mouth was full of dirt. Or worse—getting used to saying stuff like that and letting first this word and then that one slip out in the cafeteria, at the lockers ...

"It's Sophie, isn't it?"

I looked up from my locker to meet Tabatha's smooth blue eyes. She put out her hand.

"With all the stress of the auditions and everything, I never did have a chance to come up and welcome you to Drama Club. You're going to add a lot—you're a good actress."

I know I stared at her for a full minute before feebly shaking her hand.

"Going to rehearsal?" she asked.

I nodded stupidly.

"I'll walk with you," she said.

We took off toward the theatre together, under the stares of people who were obviously flabbergasted to see Tabatha Peters with me, of all people.

"I hear you're having some problems with the language in the script," she said.

"News travels fast," I said.

"It's a small department. I just wanted to tell you that, no matter what Eric or any of those guys say, I admire you for having such strong convictions."

I could feel my eyes widening.

"If it's against your beliefs to swear on stage, then I think it's neat that you won't do it. I know it'll be hard to give up the role—but, wow, there's got to be some real satisfaction in standing up for your principles like that."

At that point, my monologue should've gone:

SOPHIE: Oh, come *on!* I'm a Christian—not a moron. This doesn't have anything to do with your admiration for my convictions. You just want my role.

Instead, I just mumbled, "Thanks," and hightailed it for the other side of the theatre.

No way, I said to myself. *No way you're getting my part, sweetheart. I don't care what I have to do, I'm going to do it.*

And then I slumped down into a seat. Being jealous, wanting revenge. Those were things I tried to avoid as a Christian, too. Maybe theatre itself was just evil. Maybe this wasn't the place for me.

But I loved it!

I was pretty close to tears when Mrs. Chesterfield clapped for us all to come to the first few rows—and I was no closer to a decision. How was I going to do a read-through?

Slowly I made my way to the front. I could feel Eric looking at me, thinking, "What's the big deal?" I could sense Tabatha's eyes, glowing with, "Just cash it in. I'll take over for you." And I could hear the voices in my head I'd heard all night. "If you don't do this role, she'll probably never cast you again. If you do it as it's written, you're no different than anyone else. Please God—which one?"

"Mrs. Chesterfield?" I said.

She looked up from the knot of people clamoring around her, and suddenly it was just her and me. All the time I'd dreamed up dialogues between us, I'd never imagined that she would walk away from four other students and say to me, "Do you need to talk, Sophie?"

But she did. While Tabatha hissed through her teeth and Eric said out of the hole, "She's a theatre baby—give her a break," Mrs. Chesterfield ushered me into a seat in the back row and smiled at me out of a wreath of graying curls. She always teased that we kids had provided the gray part.

"I thought you might want to talk," she said. "Eric tells me you're struggling with KATHIE's language. Come to any decision yet?"

It looked like the only decision I'd come to was to cry. Tears were streaming down my face in a matter of seconds.

"I want this role more than anything," I said, "but I can't hear myself saying some of those words. They aren't right."

"No, they aren't," Mrs. Chesterfield said.

I choked on a sob.

"I have struggled with this issue for hours myself, Sophie. I don't swear, either, and I don't allow my students to do it in the theatre. But at the same time, a girl like KATHIE does. Can you imagine a kid with her upbringing, sitting in a detention center because she's beaten someone up to get money for drugs, saying, "Oh, shucks, what am I going to do now?""

I gave a wobbly laugh.

"We'd all be laughed off the stage and never make our point," Mrs. Chesterfield sighed. "And yet I don't want to offend anyone in the audience, or, worse, put a student actor in a compromising position."

I know I was openly staring. My mouth was hanging open, for sure, because I could taste the tears dripping into it.

"My plan was to make changes," she went on. "I thought I was going to have to do that by myself—I mean, this crowd—" she motioned toward the rest of the cast, who were now performing pieces from Monte Python for each other—"will probably want to add *more* swearing to it!" She patted my hand. "But maybe you and I together can replace the swearing—with art. I think with your ability, you can give the role power in non-verbal ways." She smiled. "That's why I cast you."

I wiped my face with both hands. "Thanks," I said.

She looked at me sadly. "I don't know if you should thank me or not," she said. "Out in the real world, you'd have had to make a choice. If you stay in theatre, someday you will."

"Then I'll tell them what you just said. I can give it power without the language. If I can't, I won't do the role."

"That's easy to say *now*," she said.

Without really meaning to, I looked down at Tabatha, who had her head buried in the script. She was probably studying KATHIE's lines already.

"I know," I said.

SCENE SIX

SOPHIE:	God—I have peace now. It's going to be OK. But why didn't you tell me that was the right choice?
GOD:	That wasn't one of the options you gave me, Sophie.
SOPHIE:	I didn't know it *was* an option!
GOD:	I know. That's why I told Mrs. Chesterfield.

SOPHIE's room is suddenly still. A calm settles over her, and she nestles her head into the pillow to dream—of costumes and convictions and applause ...

And you want to know something? That's exactly how it happened.

Crushed

Why are you bummed out today?

Because you keep writing me these stupid notes!

I'm serious. I know what your problem is. You need a guy.

I don't need a guy.

Yes, you do. You need to like somebody. There must be somebody.

I stuck Brandi's note in my chorus folder and looked up at Mr. Lewis. Why he never caught Brandi and me passing notes in sixth-period chorus I couldn't figure out. One of these days he was going to apprehend one of them and read it to the class. Then everybody in ninth-grade chorus would know I didn't "like somebody," my life would be over, and I would lie down and die.

Brandi nudged me with her elbow. I ignored her and concentrated on the alto part Mr. Lewis was pounding out on the piano.

"You have to start somewhere," she whispered to me.

"Mine eyes have seen the glory ..." I sang in her face.

She rolled her eyes.

When the bell rang, Brandi grabbed my arm. "Come on. I want to be at the locker when Keith goes by."

I pulled away. "I have to stay after."

"Oh," she said, and darted out of the room. She definitely had her priorities.

I puffed out a sigh of relief and slowly gathered up my books. I couldn't deal with Brandi's 153rd lecture about how I needed to "like somebody." The whole time she was talking I'd be remembering that she was curvy and I was a twig. That she had cultured pearls for teeth and I had a mouth full of tinsel. That she was on her 77th boyfriend and I had yet to see what the big deal was about having even *one*.

"You don't get butterflies over *anybody?*" she would ask me for the 153rd time.

And for the 153rd time I would mumble, "No."

"Kelsey, can I help you?"

I looked up. Mr. Lewis had one foot up on the riser below me, leaning lazily on his knee.

"No, sir," I said. "I was just, you know, hanging out."

He smiled and stood up. "Well, you just 'hang out' here any-time."

I tried to smile back but my mouth wouldn't do its thing. Mr. Lewis cocked his head.

"What's up, Kels?" he asked.

"What do you mean?" I said.

"You've always got a smile. I don't see one today. Can I help?"

I shrugged and thought guiltily of all the clandestine notes I'd tucked into my chorus folder while he was trying to teach.

"Friend trouble?" he asked.

"Could you tell?"

He just nodded.

"Yeah. It's friend trouble," I said. "A friend who's got a lot more going for her than I do."

He smiled. "I don't know who this person is, but there's no way she's a better alto than you are. And I don't know anybody in here with a better attitude or more mature manners. You're a natural, Kelsey. You're special. Don't forget that."

He smiled at me, and I smiled back from the door.

"See you tomorrow," he said.

"OK," I said. At least, I think it was me talking. My voice sounded different. I walked out—different. Because what I was feeling was different from anything I'd ever felt before.

I was pretty sure it was because, finally, I liked somebody.

Brandi was right. "Liking somebody" did change things. I couldn't concentrate on writing my English composition that night because my pen kept writing "ERNIE LEWIS" instead of "Shakespeare's plays live on because ..."

I lost count doing sit-ups in P.E. the next day because all I could hear in my head was his voice saying, "You're special. Don't forget that."

Man, I didn't even feel like eating *lunch*.

By sixth period chorus, Brandi had it figured out—at least, part of it.

You're acting weird today. You don't mean—

I glanced at Mr. Lewis, but he was rehearsing the tenors. I bent carefully over the paper.

OK, OK. I like somebody.

Brandi let out a squeal and plastered her hand over her mouth. Mr. Lewis looked up, and I could feel my face going turnip-colored. But he smiled at me and went back to the tenors. Brandi started writing like a crazed poet.

Who is it?

I shook my head. Her eyes sparkled. She loved intrigue.

You've got so much neat stuff ahead of you. He'll write you notes and call you. You guys'll hold hands ...

There was more but I could hardly absorb it all. All I knew was that when everybody left after class, I was staying.

"Need any help filing music?" I said to Mr. Lewis when the room was empty.

"I'll owe you forever if you can get this pile right here to disappear," he said.

"No problem," I said—in my new voice.

I guess I got all the music in the right places. It was hard, though, between watching Mr. Lewis move around the room and thinking about all the things Brandi had written.

> **Kelsey**, he would write, I just wanted to tell you again
> that you're special.

"Is Kelsey home?" he'd say on the phone in his wonderful baritone.

"Kels?"

I jerked my head back from the window I must have been staring out of.

"Yes, sir?" I said.

He smiled. "Oh, I love those manners."

I smiled back. Yeah. I was happy.

We weren't five minutes into practicing "The Battle Hymn of the Republic" the next day when the note slid across my music.

> **What's going on with you-know-who?**

I kept my eyes on Mr. Lewis' tempo arm and shrugged.

> **Nothing?**

I nodded. She could hardly stand it. When Mr. Lewis started going over a snag with the basses, she lit into me.

"So when are you going to make your move?" she whispered.

"What move?"

She huffed impatiently. "It's obvious this mystery guy is *way* shy. If you want anything to happen, *you're* going to have to make the first move."

My eyes wandered slowly from her to Mr. Lewis and back

again. "Like what?" I asked.

But Mr. Lewis tapped his baton on the music stand. "OK, folks," he said. "Let's try it all together."

"I'll tell you later," Brandi mouthed.

I stayed after class again but it was harder than ever to file the new stack of stuff Mr. Lewis gave me. All I could think of was the phrase, "make your move."

I thought about Mr. Lewis every waking moment—and the night before I'd even had a dream about him. So now I was supposed to—what? Tell him I had a crush on him? That I couldn't wait to grow up and graduate so we could go out? That he could write me a note just about anytime now?

"Kelsey!"

I jumped, and a three-inch stack of sheet music slid off the piano onto the floor.

Mr. Lewis grinned at it from his office door. "Leave it for now," he said. "If you're in the real world today—"

"I am!" I said. I could have sliced my cheeks off for turning as purple as I knew they were.

"I don't know. I had to call your name three times."

"I'm sorry …"

"Come in here a minute."

Heart slamming like a set of cymbals, I followed him into his office. *Maybe he's going to "make the move,"* I thought crazily. *What do I do? Brandi, where are you when I need you?*

Mr. Lewis was rifling through the desk drawer when I got there. With a grin like a slice of cantaloupe he handed me something he pulled out.

It was a picture of a young woman—a beautiful young

woman—with perfect teeth and great cheekbones and curves that never ended.

"Since you're a friend of mine," Mr. Lewis said, "I want to share some news with you."

I looked up stupidly from the picture.

"That's Pat," he said, still grinning until I thought he'd split. "She and I are going to get married this summer."

"Oh," I said. That was all. It's hard to talk when your mouth is frozen into a smile.

"It's still pretty much a secret," he said. "You're one of the few people who know."

"Great," I managed to say.

It was the worst evening of my life so far. I got all the way through my English composition without wanting to write a single "ERNIE LEWIS" across the page. I listened to the radio while I fell asleep, and all I heard were the songs. There were no funny little Mr. Lewis sentences running through to take me off somewhere. There wasn't anything to dream about now. I stuck my face in my pillow and cried.

Naturally, the minute I got to school the next day, Brandi made a beeline for me, with Keith right on her heels like a puppy fresh out of obedience school. One of them had obviously "made the move."

"Hi!" Brandi said. "How—"

I shot her a look that stopped her mid-syllable.

"Oh." She glanced at Keith. "We can talk later."

"Right," I said.

"Come on, Keith," she said.

But Keith was looking at me like he hadn't seen me since the day in fifth grade when I'd beat him at tether ball.

"What?" Brandi said, nudging him.

"Did you do your hair different or something?" he said to me.

"No, she didn't." Brandi tugged impatiently at his hand.

"Oh." Keith shrugged. "Well, you look, I don't know— different—good."

Brandi dragged him off down the hall, and for a long time I stared after them.

I'd been wearing my hair the same way since eighth grade. But maybe Keith was right. I was different somehow. I sighed sadly. Now I'd known a feeling I hadn't ever known before. Now I had "liked somebody," and even though it had been dumb and short and—what did they call it in English class? Unrequited. Just because I'd felt it, I wasn't ever going to be the same again.

I didn't want to go to sixth-period choir that day. I didn't want a note from Brandi, and I didn't want to see Mr. Lewis— the engaged Mr. Lewis who wasn't going to wait for me to graduate so he could hold my hand.

But I went, and I saw him, and Brandi immediately scooted a note across my folder.

Well—?

For a minute I could feel tears starting to crawl up the back of my throat. I looked away to blink them back, and there was Mr. Lewis looking at me. His eyes said, "You OK, Kels? You're special, now. Don't forget that."

I smiled. He smiled. And then he turned to the sopranos.

Forget it, I wrote to Brandi. It wasn't meant to be.
Bummer.
Nah, I wrote back, it's OK.

I couldn't write the rest. She wouldn't get it. Instead, I looked at Mr. Lewis waving his tempo arm at the sopranos and made a mental note.

I liked somebody, he didn't like me back and I lived to tell about it. I guess you have to start somewhere.

Snowbound

It really didn't matter to me.

It could snow till next February as far as I was concerned, and I could lie on the sofa in the cabin and grab some chips out of the bag Mikey was carrying every time he went by—and I'd be perfectly happy.

I guess that's why even though my name is Kent, the kids in my youth group call me C.P. (yeah, for Couch Potato).

But the fact that the six of us had sold enough stationery to keep the little old ladies in our church in thank-you notes for the rest of their natural lives—just to earn enough money to come to New England for a whole weekend of skiing—and the fact that it had been snowing so hard all night you couldn't see to walk two feet, much less ski that far, and the fact that we were stuck in a nine-hundred-square-foot cabin—*that* was driving everyone else in the group right up the wall.

"When's Phil coming back?" Brenda said. Her voice coiled up my spinal column like a bread wrapper twist tie. Man, that girl could whine.

"I haven't picked him up on radar," Evan said, "but mental

telepathy tells me he's stuck in town—and he can't get back up the hill to us—and we could be here into eternity. AHHHH!"

He lunged at her with the curtain rod he'd found in the corner and had been playing with all morning, but Brenda just stuck her tongue out at him. We were all used to him stuffing his mouth with Ping-Pong balls and stuff like that. "Creative," Phil called him.

"I hope he brings more food. I'm hungry."

"He isn't going to get back up here until it stops snowing, Mikey," Laura said. She grabbed the empty chip bag from him and peered into it. "Besides, you've been eating ever since we got up. You can't be hungry."

Deanna snorted from the corner by the fireplace. "He has the expanding capabilities of an anaconda."

"Do not," Mikey said, and then turned to Evan. "What's an anaconda?"

I didn't listen to Evan's explanation, except for a second when he slithered down the banister. I was watching Laura because I knew any minute she was going to take the situation in hand. She always did.

"I want to go skiing," Brenda said, plopping herself down next to Mikey on one of the overstuffed chairs that looked a lot like him.

"Who doesn't?" Deanna said. "You know, you can whine longer than Mikey can stuff his face—it's incredible."

"Now that's an interesting statement, Deanna," Evan said, poising the curtain rod at his lips. "Would you care to comment on that?"

She smacked at the rod coming toward her like an Oprah

Winfrey microphone and glared at Evan. "Do you know what a turkey you are?"

He immediately began to waddle and gobble, of course, and Brenda whined louder about the snow, and Mikey opened a package of Double–Stuff Oreos. Laura didn't disappoint me. She jumped up on the hearth, eyes sparkling, and spread her hands in front of her the way she always did when she had a "scathingly brilliant idea."

"Oh, no," Deanna moaned. "She's got an idea."

"I do." Laura wiggled her eyebrows mischievously at us. "Want to hear it?"

"Yeah," I said.

"He speaks!" Deanna said, but Evan poked her with the curtain rod and she shut up.

"OK—here's what we do to pass the time until Phil comes back or it stops snowing. It's a game I've always wanted to try, and now's the perfect time."

Brenda wrinkled her nose. "This sounds childish."

Laura ignored her. "Each of us writes down a question we've always wanted to ask people and have never had the guts to— you know, because our parents have told us it isn't polite to be nosy."

"It isn't," Mikey said.

"Then," Laura went on, "we each draw a question and we have to answer it—honestly."

Deanna rolled her eyes. "I don't want everybody knowing a bunch of stuff about me."

For once I had to agree with her, although, in my case, there wasn't a whole lot to know. How many secrets can you have when you're horizontal in front of a TV 30 percent of the day? How many different sequined gowns Vanna White has, maybe?

"Aw, come on," Evan said. "This could be cool. We don't have to get heavy." He tapped Mikey's Oreo bag with the curtain rod. "What do you say, guy?"

Mikey grunted. Laura took it for a yes. She looked around expectantly.

Brenda started to say, "Well, I don't know," but Deanna flipped her hair in exasperation and said, "Oh, let's just do it."

Laura looked at me, and I nodded. Of course, she could have asked me to write her next two term papers for her and I'd have nodded.

"OK!" she said, and handed out paper and pencils, then grabbed the ski cap that was waiting expectantly on Mikey's head to put our questions in. The rest of us looked at each other with uh-ohs on our faces. I wrote something down, but I knew it was stupid.

"Now," Laura said, looking around at all of us the way English teachers do the first day of school. "Who's first? Kent?"

If she weren't the only one who didn't call me C.P.—plus a lot of other reasons—I would have said, "no way." But I got to a halfway vertical position and reached in the hat.

"How can you put your hand in there?" Brenda asked.

"What do you think, the dandruff's going to attack him and rot his hand off before he pulls it out?" Evan grinned. "What a concept!"

I was staring at the slip of paper in front of me. "Can it be more than one question?" I asked.

Laura looked right at Evan. "It was *supposed* to be just one. Read them, Kent."

"Do you pick your nose?" I read.

There was a chorus of "Sick!" and "Oh, gross me out one time!" but I read on.

"Do you roll the toothpaste tube from the bottom or squeeze it in the middle? Do you say excuse me when you burp even when no one's in the room?" I let out a long sigh of relief. They were dumb questions, but at least I didn't have to unzip my soul.

"Well?" Deanna said.

"Yes. Roll. No," I said.

Brenda's voice spiraled up. "You have to give more than one-word answers."

But Laura stuck the hat in Mikey's face. He dug in like it was a bag of corn chips, but when he read the question, his face turned the color of Cream of Wheat.

"Are you afraid to die?" he read.

There was sobering silence.

I thought we weren't going to get heavy," Evan said, rubbing his freckles. "That question weighs two tons."

"Answer it, Mikey," Laura said.

He picked up the now defunct Oreo package and put it down again. "I guess I am," he said finally. "I mean, who isn't scared when they don't know what's gonna happen?"

"Why don't you know?" Deanna asked. "You go to church. You've heard about heaven. Jesus is waiting for you. What's scary about that?"

We all stared at her. For a cynic, she was sounding pretty biblical.

Evan nudged his curtain rod at Mikey's stomach. "He's just

afraid there won't be any refrigerators in heaven."

We all laughed, but I think I saw a look of panic cross Mikey's face.

"Next," Laura said. "Brenda."

"How come *you* get to decide who goes next all the time?" Brenda asked, putting her fingers gingerly into the hat.

"Just read it."

"Do you really believe in Christ and God and all that?" Brenda looked up with decision. "Whoever wrote this question, Christ isn't spelled K-R-I-S-T."

Mikey glared at her the hardest.

"So," Evan said. "Do you?"

She looked like she was going to get defensive, but then her eyes tilted down to her hands in her lap. "Most of the time I do," she said. "But then other times it's really hard because, you know, I can't see Him, and then when my parents start fighting and nobody asks me out and my dad yells at me, I think, if God were really there, He wouldn't let that bad stuff happen to me."

I saw Deanna's eyes roll, but a look from Laura stopped them on the second time around.

"I guess everybody has doubts now and then," Laura said.

"I do." Evan was pumping the curtain rod like it was a barbell, but I could tell he was serious—at least as serious as he ever gets. "I hate it when the pastors say, 'This is the way it is because it says so in the Bible, and we're telling you it's true because we've been to seminary and we know.' I mean, come on."

"I hate that, too," Laura said. "But I believe it because I've seen it for myself."

Brenda's eyes got to dinner plate size. "What—Jesus came

into your room one day or something?" Deanna couldn't suppress a snort.

"No. I mean, a lot of bad stuff happens to me, too, but there's so much more that's good, and it gets even better when God and I are really talking a lot."

"I guess if you didn't believe, what would be the point in even going on any further?" Evan said, and then he stabbed at his chest with the curtain rod.

"Could we go on to the next question?" Deanna asked.

"You pick, Evan," Mikey said.

Naturally he had to make a big deal of sticking the curtain rod into the hat and trying to skewer a slip of paper, until finally Laura just shoved one at him.

But when he read it, I saw his jaw muscles kink up.

"So read it," Deanna said.

"Are you really who you act like you are?" He stuffed the paper in his pocket and tried for a laugh. The joke fell like an egg. "Of course," he said. "I'm just a crazy guy."

There was a funny quiet, and then Deanna said, softly, "Liar."

Evan's head snapped around. "Who died and made you judge?"

Deanna straightened her shoulders and looked right at Evan. "Do you know in eighth grade when we were in that Modern Living class and we did those role plays and you played the kid that was really messed up and you cried for real right in the play? From then until the next day when you started being your usual weirdo self again, I actually had a crush on you."

Mikey stopped going at an apple in mid-bite. The rest of us tried to keep our chins from dropping to our chests.

"Personally, I think the kid who could cry is who you *really* are," Deanna said. "I think you hurt a lot of times and you try to be a clown to cover it up." She suddenly looked embarrassed. "That's just what I think."

What I thought was that Deanna still had a crush on Evan—but then, what did I know? Besides, I was getting a little nervous because my question hadn't been asked yet. The rest of them had been so good—I knew they were going to laugh mine right out into the snow.

Deanna cleared her throat—hard enough to evict a whole family of frogs—and reached for the hat. "I might as well go."

We all waited like it was a funeral. Funny how we always depended on Evan to lighten up bad moments, and when he didn't, they stayed bad.

"What's it say, Dean?" Brenda asked.

For a few minutes, Deanna looked almost nice, but the sneer slipped back onto her face as she looked up from her slip of paper. "Somebody really had a nerve," she said. "Listen to this: 'Have you ever told a lie that backfired so bad you had to keep lying?'"

Deanna stared at the paper, and I seriously considered pretending to fall asleep. Evan was right. These questions did weigh two tons.

But just as I was about to nod off, Deanna said, "Look, you guys. If I answer this question, I mean honestly, it means I'm telling you something I've never told another living soul. Can you deal with that?"

We all nodded solemnly, even me. When she looked at Evan, he said, "You don't have to answer it if you don't want to. This isn't *Judge Judy* or anything."

But she shook her head. "Everybody else has been honest. And if I can't trust you guys, who can I trust?"

For a minute, I almost liked her.

"OK." Deanna took a deep breath, like she was about to go under. Maybe she was.

"Last year, I was up for that summer scholarship to Japan—"

"You got it. You went!" Brenda said.

"Yeah—I went. And my parents—they were so proud—I mean, I do all this academic stuff for them because if I don't, it's like they hate me."

She rolled her eyes, only this time I was pretty sure it was to get rid of the tears that were starting to collect.

"When it got down to the final interviews, I was up against this other girl. I was sure she was going to get it. We had the same grades, same number of activities and honors, but I knew when it got down to it, she could come across warmer and nicer and all that stuff they want so you can be a junior ambassador while you're there. I just can't do that."

None of us disagreed, but Evan went over and sat next to her.

"If I didn't make it, my parents would give me grief for months and I couldn't take that. So—" she stopped. The rolling eyes weren't working on the tears anymore. "So I spread a rumor about her and hoped the committee would get wind of it, and they did."

"What was the rumor?" Mikey asked.

"I don't think we need to know that."

I'd have expected that to come from Laura, but it was Evan who said it. "So you've been walking around with that on your head since last spring?" he asked. His voice was husky.

She just nodded and cried. I kind of wanted to do the same.

"Go ahead, you guys!" she said. "Tell me what a witch I am. Throw me out of the group." She was crying so hard now, she could barely talk.

But then an amazing thing happened. Evan reached over and put his arm around her. "How does that thing go?" he asked. "Let he who is without sin cast the first stone?"

"We've all done stuff like that, Dean," Laura said.

"I bet you never have," Mikey said.

Brenda nodded. "You're practically perfect, Laura."

Well, that was one for Brenda in my book.

Laura turned a pretty good shade of magenta and snatched up the ski cap. "I guess it's my go," she said.

That's when it occurred to me, slow learner that I am, that Laura was going to get my question—my stupid question. I tried to make myself one with the couch, but her eyes still flickered over at me for a second after she read it.

"Are you afraid," she read, "I mean, really afraid of what people think of you?"

"Oh, that's a great question for you," Brenda said sarcastically. "Why should you be afraid?"

But Laura was shaking her head at Brenda. I was watching Laura's face and slowly coming to a sitting-up position.

"I am not perfect," Laura said. "Let me tell you, I am so gross sometimes."

"Do you pick your nose?" Evan said, grinning. Deanna smacked him, but she left her hand on his arm.

"I mean it. I can be so bossy and so overbearing and so dom-ineering."

"Don't stop there," Deanna said. But she was smiling, too. For some reason, we all were.

"I always take over. I give people advice I don't take myself. I'm not even sure who I am—and it's like other people's opin-ions determine who I think I'm supposed to be."

"I don't believe that." Everyone stared at me because I was the one who said it.

"What did you say, C.P.?" Evan said.

By then there was no point in saying my usual, "Oh noth-ing," or just spacing out. They weren't going to go for that now, not after this day.

I took a deep breath and started talking, but I couldn't look at Laura. "It doesn't matter what people think about you, you're always the same. You're always nice, and you don't put people down or expect them to live up to your way of doing stuff. You always make everything right when the rest of us are messed up."

The fact that I had never said more than two sentences in a row on a given evening in front of this or any other group of more than two people may account for the fact that all of them stared at me like I was newly arrived from Uranus.

I think Evan said, "Didn't know you cared, guy," and I think somebody else put in, "That was a neat thing to say."

But Laura's was the only voice I really heard. She just said, "Thank you, Kent. That really helped me."

And when I looked up, there were tears shining in her eyes.

Not too long after that, it stopped snowing and we made popcorn and Mikey ate most of it. Then Phil came back and we did go skiing and I actually went down the bunny hill with Laura. Being on skis isn't much like being on a couch, but I made it.

Later we went home and most of us went back to being who we were before.

Except Brenda was baptized.

And Evan and Deanna started going out.

And Laura and I—we're helping each other stop worrying about what other people think.

Mikey? He just eats and smiles. But I think, like the rest of us, he remembers the day we played Laura's game.

Bringing
Up
Good
Parents

The Smother Mother

I kid you not—it started before my buns even made contact with the kitchen chair. Before I could even curl my lip at my oatmeal, Mom started in.

"Noel, what do you have on your mouth?" she said.

Uh, lips? I thought.

Smile.

"Lip gloss," I said.

Mom put a glass of fresh-squeezed orange juice next to my oatmeal bowl and sighed—the way she does—from her toes or someplace.

"We have had this conversation two hundred times," she said. "No makeup. Go wipe it off."

But I'll look like a twelve-year-old.

Grimace.

"Mom, it's just a little lip gloss. Katie Whalen gets to wear blush, for Pete's sake, and she's the *pastor's* kid, and a whole *year* younger than me …"

"I'm not Katie Whalen's mother—I'm yours. Go."

I did.

Mom was a little off on her calculations. We'd had that conversation—or some facsimile thereof—about two *thousand* times. Just in the previous twenty-four hours there had been:

"Mom, can I go shopping with Amy? They're having a sale at Macy's—"

"You and I are going shopping Saturday. I'll get you what you want."

OK—let's try another approach.

Sigh.

"Can't I just get something on my own? I have babysitting money—"

"You know Amy. She'll talk you into some micro-mini thing we'll end up having to take back. Tell her I said no."

I did.

Then there was:

"What are you reading, Noel?"

"*Don't Count on Homecoming Queen*. It's by Nancy—"

"Have I read that?"

Aw, man—here we go again.

Eye roll.

"No, but I got it from the library at school."

"Let me look at it."

"Mom! Why do you send me to a Christian school if you don't even trust their librarians?"

"Are you getting smart with me?"

"No, Ma'am."

"Let me look at it."

I did.

Just since the day before, we'd had clone-conversations

about me having my door closed when Amy came over (you shouldn't be talking about anything you wouldn't want a mother to hear, Noel, so why do you need to have the door shut?) and me wanting to call Andy Carlson about algebra homework (you don't call boys, Noel) and my wanting to try out for *Grease* (I've seen that movie, Noel; the theme isn't proper).

Every time, I thought about what I'd *like* to say—and then I rolled my eyes, curled my lip, sighed, or did all of the above.

And then I did whatever she told me to do. Arguing was out of the question, which was why I vented to my best friend Amy Robbins about twenty times a day.

"I don't know how you stand it," Amy said that morning on the bus when I'd unloaded about the lip gloss discussion. She pulled a lipstick out of her backpack and smeared it on. "My parents are strict, but good grief—"

"Your parents are not strict, girl," I said. "You don't know what strict is."

"Uh-*huh*," she said, fudgy-brown eyes popping out of her head. "No single car dates 'til I'm sixteen. Curfew at 11:00 on weekends. No going out on school nights, period."

I shoved my fingers back through my hair. "If those were the only rules my mother had, I'd be, like, the happiest person on the planet. I don't mind that stuff—it's the you-can't-go-to-the-mall-without-me, don't-try-on-clothes-you-have-no-intention-of-buying, don't-look-at-a-boy-unless-he-looks-at-you-first—all that stuff—that's what makes me want to scream!"

"So scream."

"Right. I'm not allowed to do that either."

Amy grinned at me over the top of her compact, blush brush

in midair. "You're gonna scream today when you see the drill team list."

I raked my hair again. "You really think I made it? Tell me honestly."

"Yeah, I think you made it. I think we both did. It's gonna be a blast."

It *was* a comforting thought. I felt so boxed in so much of the time, it would be nice to have something to really look forward to everyday. Practices before school. Performing at games—of which Friendship Christian School had about a jillion a week. Wearing a cool uniform.

And Amy was right. My name was at the top of the list, right before hers.

"I'm so jazzed I can hardly stand it!" she said as she danced around in the hall in front of the bulletin board like she had to go to the bathroom.

I wasn't much more controlled, especially after the meeting we had with our advisor at lunch when we got the picture of what our uniforms were going to look like.

"These are *cool!*" I whispered to Amy.

"With your legs, you're gonna look amazing in this," she whispered back.

We gazed at the photo of the girl in the white boots and the green little-boy shorts and the sharp-looking jacket (that promised to make even *my* waist look tiny) until I thought we'd wear the thing out.

My mother, however, was less than impressed. I don't know why it surprised me when I got home, announced that I'd made it, put the picture on the kitchen table—and she said, "Noel, you are *not* going to wear that."

I stared at her. "Well, yeah, Mom—it's our uniform."

"You're not wearing shorts that short."

"Well, *we* might not wear them that short—I mean, it's a Christian school—"

"I know what it is—I write the check for your tuition every month—and I'm going to talk to Mr. Hess about this."

Could this get any more embarrassing?

Controlled breath.

"Mom—this is really important to me."

"And it's important to me that you maintain your modesty."

"Mom!"

"Noel, that's enough."

Then it was her turn to sigh. She put her hands on my shoulders, and her eyes softened. "Why don't you go up and see what I got you today? It's on your bed. I think it'll make you feel better."

If it wasn't a drill team uniform, it had no chance of making me feel one ounce better. And it wasn't. The outfit spread across my bed like a department store window display was a khaki skirt and a white blouse, both from the Gap. I snatched them up, flung open my closet door, and hurled them into the back corner. Then as soon as I heard Mom leave for the grocery store, I called Amy.

"From the Gap?" Amy said. "Cool. I wish my mom would buy me stuff there."

"That isn't the point! How come she can go alone and pick out clothes for me and expect me to like them, but I can't be trusted to go out on my own and pick out stuff for myself?"

"Yeah—"

"And now she wants to pick out the drill team uniform! This is so embarrassing. I'm just gonna drop out of the team." I raked my hair with both sets of fingers. "I am so sick of this!"

"Not as sick of it as I am."

I stopped. "What do you mean?"

"I'm sick of listening to you vent about your mother when you never do anything about it."

I stared into the phone. "What am I supposed to do? If I argue I get grounded for like a semester."

"Don't argue. Just do one thing without your mother's permission, just to see how it feels."

"What?" I said. "You mean, like sneak out on a date or something?"

"Do you *want* to do that?"

I shook my now completely trashed hair. "No. I get the reason for that rule. What I don't get is why I can't, like, go to the mall, for Pete's sake!"

"So, let's go."

I felt a chill. "You mean, without telling her?"

"Sure. It's Friday. Don't your parents usually go out on Friday nights?"

"Yeah, with the Marshalls. They do Mexican food."

"Cool. So, when they're gone, you and I will just—go to the mall."

"She'd say I was asking for trouble."

"You don't tell her, idiot. You just do it. Just to prove to yourself that you're not your mother's clone—you're you."

I felt the chill again, and I knew what it was. It was the thrill of deceit quivering in my little veins.

"OK," I said. "What time?"

We put together a plan that would've made James Bond eat his heart out. As it turned out, all we had to do when my parents left the house was go to the corner, get on the bus, and ride to Crestview Mall. Then, basically, I broke every one of my mother's five thousand commandments.

We walked around the mall, just to be walking around. (*There's no purpose to that, Noel.*)

We tried on clothes. (*That's ridiculous if you don't plan to buy them!*)

We shared an order of French fries. (*Do NOT put that junk in your body!*)

We sat in the center of the mall at the fountain and discreetly boy-watched. (*Nice girls do not need to be thinking about boys.*)

And when a couple of guys came by and asked us if we wanted to go to a good party, we said no thanks and moved smoothly on.

"See?" Amy said to me as we headed for the restroom. "You're not some airhead who doesn't know how to take care of herself. Aren't you having fun?"

"Yeah," I said. And I was—until the next second when the toilet stall door opened and Mrs. Whalen stepped out.

Suddenly it didn't matter that *she* let *her* kid wear blush—I felt like I'd been nabbed by the Parent Police.

Amy slithered into a stall before Mrs. Whalen saw her. Me, I just stood there turning red to the roots of my hair and breaking into a cold, guilty sweat.

"Well, hi, Noel!" she said pleasantly. She looked around the room. "Where is your mother?"

"Um—she's out having Mexican food," I said. I was sure Amy was groaning to herself in the stall, but I couldn't lie. I wasn't allowed to.

"Ah," Mrs. Whalen said. She smiled faintly. "So, while the cat's away, the mice will play, huh?"

I nodded stupidly. "Yes, Ma'am," I said.

Please, please don't tell my mom you saw me here! I wanted to plead—while getting on my knees and hanging on her arm.

I didn't, of course. I didn't have to. She was looking right into my eyes, and I just knew she was about to handcuff me and take me straight to Los Tres Amigos or whatever it was called. But she surprised me. She brushed her hand across my shoulder and said, "Suppose I call you tomorrow and we go out for a Coke? After I ask your mom, of course."

"Of course," I said.

So much for the guilty pleasures of roaming the mall unchaperoned. As soon as Amy came out of the stall we hightailed it for the bus and went home. I was in my house way before my parents were even eating their sopapillas, I'm sure, and they didn't even ask me what I'd done all evening.

Still, I couldn't sleep that night, and when the phone rang about ten o'clock the next morning, I about jumped out of my skin. When Mom started using her I'm-talking-to-the-pastor's-wife voice, I knew it was Mrs. Whalen, and I started making plans for what I was going to do in my room for the next eighteen weeks.

But Mom was smiling when she got off the phone, and she

said, "Isn't that nice? Mrs. Whalen wants to take you out for a Coke. Why don't you wear that new outfit I bought you?"

Out of sheer guilt, I did. It poked me at every joint, and I felt like a big pincushion by the time Mrs. Whalen came and picked me up. I wasn't sure I could handle the inevitable lecture I was going to get about honoring my father and mother. I didn't really need it. I was already resigned to a life of social sterility until I was eighteen.

"Too early for Baskin Robbins?" she said when I climbed into the car.

"That's fine," I said.

Might as well pig out on my last meal before I go into solitary confinement.

Stiff smile.

"Relax, Noel," she said. "I'm not going to give you a hard time. You look like you've been punishing yourself all night."

All I could do was stare straight-ahead—dumbfounded—until we went through the drive-in. I had a chocolate blast in my hand, and we wandered out into the park. Mrs. Whalen sat down at a cement table, and I followed suit.

Then she poked her spoon into her yogurt and said, "Was that the first time you slipped out and did your own thing behind your parents' back?"

I nodded miserably.

"I'm impressed," she said.

"You are?"

"Oh, yeah. I was doing it by about age twelve, myself."

"You?"

Mrs. Whalen grinned into her yogurt. "My mother had a set

of rules for me—well, let's just say a lot like your mom's. She wouldn't let me get my ears pierced. I wasn't allowed to wear jeans—"

"No way!"

"Way. Oh, and no dating until I was eighteen."

"Eighteen!"

"Oh, yeah. I knew women in convents who had more freedom. Naturally, I went off to college and just went wild."

I set my blast aside, full of delicious indignation. "See what she made you do!" I said.

"Actually, no," she said. "She didn't do it to me—I did it to myself."

I didn't get it.

"Yes, she was much too protective," Mrs. Whalen said. "And I probably wouldn't have rebelled like that if she hadn't been. But I made the choices myself. You have choices, too."

"I know," I said. I abandoned the chocolate blast completely. "After last night, I guess I have to choose to just follow the rules and be miserable."

I glanced at her sideways, half-hoping she'd have some other alternative for me. To my disappointment, she just nodded sympathetically.

"Believe me, I know how hard it is," she said.

I had an idea. "Could you talk to my mother?" I asked. "Maybe get her to lighten up on some of that stuff?"

"Absolutely not," Mrs. Whalen said. "I'm not going to get into telling your mother how to parent. I don't even think I should tell you what I do and don't agree with that your mother does. You understand that, right?"

I sagged, but I nodded.

"However, here's a ray of hope," she said. "You're miserable now—so much so at times that I'm pretty sure you won't be as sad as a lot of people are when it's time to leave home. You'll be ready to get out and spread your wings. You'll be more excited than you are afraid."

"That's for sure."

Mrs. Whalen put her hand on my arm. "But until then, Noel, don't be a fool. Honor your mother. Learn what you can from her—and I'm sure there's plenty she has to teach."

"I guess."

"Be patient. Make your plans for the future." She grinned. "Pray a lot."

"Uh, for sure."

"I'm serious. Concentrate on what God has in store for you when the time comes to go. And let me tell you something else."

I was starting to get interested. "OK," I said.

"Your mother isn't going to want you to leave, you know that."

"Uh-huh."

"But that's OK, because leaving is *your* job. It even says so in the Bible."

"Where?" I was ready to break out the King James and commit it to memory.

"In Genesis, it doesn't say a parent shall let go of her child. It says a man—or in this case woman—shall leave his mother. You'll be ready to do the leaving if you use this time to prepare. You'll know how to fly because you've been training with God." Her face grew serious. "But until then, no sneaking around, Noel. You're too good for that."

I looked down at my fingernails. It was all making sense. Too much sense. "Should I tell her about my trip to the mall?" I asked.

She looked into her yogurt again. "If she asks. But you'd better tell God and see what He says. He's your best ally from now on."

There was a lot to think about, and I was pretty quiet as Mrs. Whalen finished up her yogurt and drove me home. When I got there, Mom was in the kitchen, putting groceries away, and her face was all soft and shiny like it got sometimes. "Go upstairs," she said. "There's a surprise for you on your bed."

Oh, let me guess.

Smile.

"Cool," I said.

I took the stairs like I had wooden legs, crossed my room, and picked up the tie-dyed cotton sweater and the wide-legged jeans and started to shove them into the back of my closet.

I don't care if she does have good taste. I don't care if they did come from Abercrombie & Fitch. I'm not wearing them—

Then I stopped in mid-fling and looked at them.

OK, maybe I wouldn't wear them—but it might be a good idea to ask God about that before I made a choice.

With a sigh I reached for a hanger. 'Til then I'd better hang them right in the middle to remind me.

"Remind you of what?" my mother would have asked. "That I'm your mother?"

No chance of forgetting that.

Sigh.

OK. Smile.

The Gag-Me Girl

'm going to gag," I said to Amber and Toni that day, second period in the library.

Toni was frowning and didn't even look up from her encyclopedia. "Bad batch of Fruit Loops this morning, Meg?" she said.

"No. Too much Carrie Schafer. Check her out."

I nodded toward the periodicals section where Carrie was gazing with reverent absorption into the face of Mrs. Pinckney, the librarian, as if the woman were imparting the ultimate secrets of the universe. Carrie was, of course, nodding just enough not to disturb the flawless blond bob that, she once told us, had never been touched with a blow-dryer or curling iron. She didn't want to risk style damage.

She wasn't as concerned about personality damage, I'd told Toni and Amber when she'd walked away. Now as I looked at my two cohorts, I knew they were waiting for my newest comment about little Miss Gag-Me.

"Pinckney wants to adopt her," I said.

Amber gave one of her trademark snorts. "She'll have to fight Ms. Barry for her."

I glanced at our English teacher, who was hurrying toward Carrie and the librarian, eyebrows lifted in delicious anticipation. "You mean old Comma Conscious?" I said. "The three of them ought to start a commune. They couldn't come up with an original thought among them."

Toni slapped the encyclopedia closed in disgust. "I can't find anything on Eleanor Roosevelt in here. Doesn't she go to our church?"

Amber blinked at her. "Eleanor Roosevelt? I don't think so."

Toni rolled her eyes. "No, Swifty. Carrie Schafer."

I groaned. "Go to our church?" I tugged at the sleeve of Toni's T-shirt. "You haven't been going there long enough to notice that she thinks she runs it."

"OK, definitely," Amber said. Her eyes started blinking faster; they did that when she got onto a subject she actually knew something about. She started ticking things off on her fingers. "She sings in the choir."

"First soprano," I put in.

"She teaches a Sunday school class—"

"Come on, Amber." I said with mock seriousness. "She invented Sunday school."

Amber frowned. "She did?"

"Never mind," Toni said, reaching for another volume of the Britannica. "I get the point."

"The doors to the church don't open but she's there," Amber went on as if Toni hadn't tried to change the subject. That was OK with me. I liked the subject.

"Not just the church doors," I said. "We're talking the parsonage doors, too."

"What's the parsonage?" Toni asked. She'd just become a Christian about a month before. She wasn't up on the vocabulary yet.

"That's where the pastor lives," Amber said. "Carrie baby-sits for Dr. Mayhew and his wife—"

"And never leaves without doing Mrs. Mayhew's dishes and folding the laundry for her," I said. "Just ask Carrie. She'll tell you herself. Along with reciting her grade point average—and her dream of finding a husband at Bible college and becoming a pastor's wife."

"Did she actually tell you that?" Amber asked.

"No—but you know she's thinking it. Look at her!"

Our heads swiveled in unison to the computer where Carrie was arranging her precisely even stack of notebooks on the stand beside her. Not a dog-eared one in the bunch.

"What I don't get," I whispered, "is what she's smiling at. Do you sit and grin at the computer screen when you're looking up magazine articles?"

"Maybe she's happy," Toni said.

"Maybe she's stuck that way is more like it," I said. "Get over it—nobody is that perfect."

Ms. Barry passed Carrie and slid her hand approvingly across her shoulder. Carrie looked up and smiled until I thought the corners of her mouth were going to slip into her ears. Then she carefully adjusted the cuffs of her crisp, plaid blouse and placed her fingertips on the keys. Even from where I was sitting I could see that her nails were shell pink. I turned to Toni to comment, but I waited. When Toni's intelligent brown eyes got that intense, I always knew she was about to come out with something good. She was the only person I knew who could be even more sarcastic than I was.

"Let me get this straight," she said. "I mean, you know, so I can get back to this research paper."

"What?" I said. It was all I could do not to lick my chops.

Toni looked me right in the eyes. "So it isn't OK for a Christian to try to be perfect—is that what you're saying?"

I could feel the expectant smirk I'd been wearing suddenly freeze on my face. "Well—no," I said.

"Then what's the problem?" Toni asked.

My initial shock was wearing off. I twitched my shoulders with the first prickles of ticked-offedness. "Are you telling me you don't think she's too good to be true?"

Toni put up both hands. "I didn't say that. I think she tries way too hard." She turned back to the book. "I'm just not all freaked out about it."

"Who's freaked out?" I said. Mrs. Pinckney glared my way, and I lowered it to a hiss. "I just don't want you thinking that to be a good Christian you have to be like that, all sugary sweet, never biting the erasers off your pencils. She just bothers me."

"Then maybe something's wrong with her," Toni said. She perused the page and scowled at it. I scowled at her.

"An overdose of Sweet 'n' Low," I muttered.

Beside me, Amber giggled nervously. Toni's eyes came up over the top of the encyclopedia and shot into me. "OK," she said. "Then maybe something's wrong with you."

If Pinckney hadn't been keeping me under such close surveillance, I'd have flung several volumes of the Britannica at her. As it was, I could feel my eyes smoldering. "You sound like my father," I said.

"Your father the therapist?" she said. Toni was completely unruffled, which only set my feathers up on end.

"Yeah," I said testily. "He's constantly analyzing everybody. I don't need to be analyzed, and neither does the Gag-Me girl. It's simple: She's a fake, and that bugs me."

Toni gave me one last look before she slapped the encyclopedia closed. "Fine," she said calmly. "You want to go to the county library tonight to work on this? I can't find what I need here."

I shook my head woodenly. I wasn't ready to change the subject yet, but there was no use pushing it with Toni. She was as stubborn as a jar lid when she didn't want to discuss something.

"My mom's out of town," I said tightly. "My dad's taking me out to dinner."

"Come by there tomorrow then," she said. "I'll probably be camped out all weekend to get this paper done." She shoved her binder into her backpack and gave me a half smile. "Happy analysis, tonight."

Fortunately, my dad wasn't in the mood to get into my head that evening as we sat across from each other at Famous Murphy's. He'd just gone online that afternoon for the first time, and he was all over it. While I was picking at my lemon chicken, he went on and on about his new e-mail address and how far he'd already traveled down the information superhighway.

"I'm using SHRINK782 as my screen name," he was saying. "And don't tell me it's cheesy. I already know. That's why I picked it—except for the numbers they stuck onto the end."

"Cool," I said miserably.

His antennae went up. I could feel them.

"Something bothering you, Meggie?"

I didn't answer him, because I wasn't really sure what it was that was sending me spiraling down into the hate-myself abyss. Ever since that conversation in the library about Carrie Schafer, I'd been feeling kind of ugly, like my lip was in a permanent curl or something. At first I thought it was because Toni had made me mad. After all, hadn't she twisted my words beyond recognition and made me sound like I was some kind of stalker because I told it like it was?

Usually self-righteous indignation pumps me up. If somebody misjudges me or misrepresents me, I can ride on it for days. But I didn't feel good about being right this time. I just couldn't figure out which part of it I was wrong about. Carrie did, after all, make me feel nauseated every time she went on about her three hours of personal daily devotions. If you asked me, she was a prime example of those dudes Jesus talked about who stood on the street corner pounding their chests and saying, "Thank you, Lord, that I am not like other men." She was a total fake. Why should I feel bad because that made my tongue itch?

"What? Am I talking to myself here?"

I snapped back to Dad, who was observing me with a practiced eye.

"Sorry," I said. "I have a lot on my mind."

"All right—what's his name?"

I rolled my eyes, and my dad laughed. At the very moment

that I was wondering how I was going to keep him from asking the inevitable how's-your-love-life, a sound rose above the steady, polite hum of restaurant conversation. Somebody was talking too loudly, too harshly, and it jarred like the tremor of an earthquake. Everybody in the place looked around while pretending not to look around, and Dad and I did too.

"You eat like a gorilla!" a woman said in a shrill voice. "I don't know why I even bother to take you out."

My eyes cut right to her, and I stifled a gasp.

"Who would bring a young child into a place like this anyway?" muttered my father, who couldn't see them.

"She isn't talking to a little kid," I said, more to myself than to him. "She's talking to Carrie Schafer."

Dad's eyebrows shot up. "Carrie Schafer who goes to our church? She must be fourteen or fifteen."

I nodded. I couldn't take my eyes off of the scene, two tables down. Carrie had her back to me, but it was unmistakably her. Nobody else I knew had that not-a-hair-out-of-place look or had posture like a gymnast ready to nail the vault. It was the woman sitting across from her, though, to whom my eyes were glued.

I'd seen Carrie's mother only a few times. She didn't go to church regularly. Carrie was always raving on about how her mom's job as a fashion buyer for Castnor Knott kept her running to Paris and Milan. And although I knew that this gaunt-looking woman with the bullet eyes was definitely Mrs. Schafer, she didn't look at all the way I'd seen her, impeccably dressed, gazing with rapt adoration from her church pew up at Carrie in choir.

This lady was yammering at Carrie like a truck driver, slurring words and practically spitting as she made mocking faces at her daughter. One hand waved in the air, almost out of control. The other was clenched like a claw around a glass of something I was pretty sure wasn't iced tea.

"A-minus?" she spat. "What—are you afraid to make an A in chemistry? Afraid you'll scare off the boys?"

Carrie shook her head. If possible, her backbone seemed to stiffen even straighter.

"You're hopeless," the woman said. She lurched up from the table, taking the corner of the tablecloth with her and pulling her plate dangerously close to the edge. "I'm going to the little girls' room," she said. "Order me another drink."

She didn't finish her sentence but stumbled, glassy-eyed, past our table. I was incredibly glad Carrie didn't turn around to watch her go, or she'd have seen the horrified look I knew was on my face. I'd never before witnessed a scene involving a drunk person abusing somebody, but I knew without a doubt that this was what it was. I looked at my dad. To my surprise, his face was not in the midst of a diagnosis. It was softly sad.

"That's a well-kept secret," he said. "I feel bad for her, worse for her daughter—Carrie, is it?"

I nodded absently and looked back at Carrie. A pang went through me. Her shoulders had sagged, a sight you never saw. And she actually ran her hand back through her perfect hair. It fell forlornly back into place, and she deliberately straightened her back and picked up her water glass as primly as ever. For a second there she'd almost been human. Then she'd caught herself.

I could feel my father watching me. "The sad part is," he said, "when they get home, she'll probably put her mother to bed because she'll barely be able to walk. And then she'll cover for her if anyone calls, and tell them she turned in with a headache. Tomorrow she'll try to be as perfect as she can be so her mother won't have a reason to get depressed and drink."

I looked at him quickly. "Really?" I asked.

"That's the way it is with a lot of children of alcoholics. They try to control an uncontrollable situation and set up impossible standards for themselves in the process." He ran his napkin across his mouth and stood up.

"Where are you going?" I asked.

"To call them a cab," he said. "Why don't you start praying?"

As he walked away, I stared at the back of Carrie's perfect head. I wasn't even sure where to start.

Just as she'd said she'd be, Toni was in the county library the next morning, ready to spend her Saturday gleaning information on Eleanor Roosevelt. I was pretty halfhearted about doing the same for Martin Luther King—or anyone else for that matter. I was too bummed to concentrate on anything. I found Toni in a corner and flopped down at the table across from her. She fanned her thumb through a stack of note cards.

"I didn't know if you were still speaking to me," she said.

"I'm barely speaking to myself," I said. "I'm such a jerk."

That got her full attention. I'm not one for putting myself down—only other people.

"The Carrie Schafer thing?" she asked.

I nodded glumly. "You know what you were saying about

how there was either something wrong with her or something wrong with me?"

"Yeah."

I shoved my cheek into my hand. "I think it was both. I found out what is wrong with her. Now I wish I knew why I'm such a miserable excuse for a Christian."

"*Now* you tell me," she said dryly. "You're the one who brought me to the Lord, remember?"

"And then I turned out to be a total hypocrite."

Toni's eyes got intense. "Don't start gagging me the way she gagged you," she said.

"What do you mean?"

"You're expecting yourself to be perfect. So your mouth gets you into trouble sometimes. Yikes, you're human. Wow."

"That doesn't make it OK."

"It does if you learned something."

I looked at her in surprise, and she shrugged. "Your dad's a therapist—my mother's a teacher. We're all at the mercy of our parents' professions."

Then she grinned inquisitively, as if waiting for me to speak.

"What did I learn?" I said.

"Yeah."

"I guess that you can't criticize somebody if you don't have all the information about why she does what she does. I can't tell you why, but Carrie's really hurting. She doesn't floss her teeth and keep her pens and pencils in a little zipper bag in her binder because she likes to."

Toni leaned across the table toward me. "Then I have a question for you," she said.

I moaned. "Last time you asked a question it opened this big old honkin' can of worms." I looked into her eyes. "You're going to ask it anyway, aren't you?"

"I know I'm just now starting my relationship with the Lord," she said, "but isn't He telling us that we're supposed to help people who are hurting?"

"Yeah," I said slowly.

"So—why aren't we helping her?"

I opened my mouth to agree, but in spite of the ache I felt for Carrie, it wouldn't come out. "She drives me nuts," I said lamely.

Toni sat back and crossed her arms over her chest. "And I'm sure we drive Jesus nuts. Especially you."

"Thanks," I said wryly.

She poked her hand into the pocket of her jeans and pulled out thirty-five cents, which she deposited on the table.

"What's that for?" I said.

Toni looked around at the library, with its books positioned precisely on their shelves. "I think this looks like Carrie Schafer's kind of fun," she said.

I let out a big old sigh and slid the change off the table. "You think the number's in the book?" I said.

As I walked away she hissed after me, "No gagging in the phone booth."

Nah, I thought. I'm pretty sure Jesus never gagged.

When THEY Came for Christmas

I didn't see why they had to come for Christmas. Aunt Karen, Uncle Dan, and their two Velcro children had always gone to Uncle Dan's mother's home in Seattle for the holidays. That meant I had to be their personal, full-time babysitter only once a year, at the family summer reunion.

But there they were, pulling into our snow-covered driveway, ready to invade our Christmas. Even from my bedroom window on the second story I could see Tad hanging out of the back of their car, pudgy face raw-red in the cold, his nappy hair sticking out in every direction. I could almost hear him bellowing, "Sammie! We're here! Can we see your room? Can I play your CDs?" And I could imagine Uncle Dan barking, "Get your head in here!"

I shuddered. My parents had always told me that the reason Tad demanded so much attention and little Amber clung to me like a cobweb was because their father yelled and threatened all the time. In fact, they'd just reminded me of that the day before.

"Why don't they go to Seattle, like usual?" I had asked at the dinner table.

"Uncle Dan's mother died," Mom said.

"So why don't they just stay home?"

"Samantha!"

I mumbled, "Sorry," and avoided looking at my father, who I knew was shooting bullets from his eyes.

"What is your problem with this?" he said.

I poked my rice pilaf with my fork. "I know they're my cousins, but they drive me nuts. Tad can't walk into my room without breaking something. The pictures start falling off my walls as soon as he comes in the door."

"He's a big boy for twelve," Mom pointed out.

"And Amber's a midget for seven, and she still manages to be everywhere I am. I feel like a mother baboon with this baby constantly clinging to my hide."

"They love you," Dad said. "With a father like theirs, they need all the love they can get."

"What about their mother?" I said as I stabbed my sirloin tips. "If they need all this love, why does she dump them on me the minute she arrives?"

Mom gave me a warning look. "Aunt Karen is exhausted. She's dealing with a learning-disabled son, an emotionally immature daughter, a husband who ..." She stopped. "She's grateful for a few minutes of peace when you're around."

"A few minutes?" I said.

"Samantha, I don't like this attitude." Dad's eyes were shooting several rounds a second. "You will not be rude to them."

"I won't be rude," I said, giving the sirloin tips another stab. "But please don't expect me to baby-sit them the entire time."

I thought I heard my mother gasp. But, surprisingly, my

father didn't turn into a semiautomatic weapon. Instead, his voice got deadly calm.

"We expect you to do whatever the family needs you to do. God started Christmas with a pathetic little family no one wanted to take in."

We finished dinner in silence.

* * * * *

It definitely wasn't silent now. Aunt Karen was greeting Mom in her bugle voice, and Amber was wailing in her shrill one, and over it all I could hear Tad howling, "Where's Sammie?"

"Sam!" Dad called from the front door. "They're here."

"No kidding," I muttered, and went downstairs.

"Sammie, thank goodness," Aunt Karen said as she hugged me. "All I've heard for a thousand miles has been, 'When are we going to see Sammie?' They'd walk right past the PlayStation to get to you."

I squeezed out a smile, despite the fact I had Tad's arms wrapped around my waist like a pair of handcuffs and Amber's wet face plastered against my thigh.

"Can we go up to your room?" Tad brayed.

"Will you read me a book?" Amber whined.

"Of course," I said, teeth gritted. "What else?"

When I opened my bedroom door, Tad plunged past me and careened against the wall, tearing a corner of my Michael W. Smith poster away from the wallpaper. He dived for my CD case, and Amber, still wrapped around my leg, pointed to my doll collection. I sighed and went toward it, hauling her like a ball and chain.

Below, the adults were gathered in the kitchen, and I could hear Aunt Karen's voice baying above everyone else's, stress wired around every syllable, with Mom and Dad's words weaving through like soothing hands.

The only dulcet tones I didn't hear were Uncle Dan's. Come to think of it, he had been strangely quiet ever since they'd arrived. Usually he downed a couple of Michelobs he'd brought in and then dominated the conversation. I glanced out the window, but their car was still there. He hadn't gone on a beer run.

"What can we do now, Sammie?" Tad said.

"How about a movie?" Mom said from the doorway.

She picked her way across my doll and CD-littered floor and tucked a wad of bills into my hand.

"Sammie will walk you down to the theatre at the mall," she said to Tad and Amber. "There's enough there for drinks and popcorn—and to take Heidi along," she added for my benefit.

She also whispered, "Thank you. Their parents really need some time."

"I need some time, too," I hissed to Heidi when we'd finally gotten settled into our seats at the movie.

Heidi nodded knowingly. She was my best friend. She'd been listening to me rant about this for weeks.

"Sammie?"

"What, Tad?" I asked, without looking back at him.

"I spilled my Coke."

"How bad is it?" I said to Heidi.

She peeked past me. "You don't want to know."

I turned to face Tad, who was holding an empty cup,

wearing half its contents and sitting in the rest.

"Ta-ad!" I said.

"I didn't mean to!" he said. And then, right there before my eyes, he cringed.

"I'm not going to hit you," I said. "Just go to the restroom and get cleaned up. And bring back some paper towels so you can clean this up."

He plowed down the row, stepping on three people's feet en route.

"Can I sit in your lap, Sammie?" Amber said.

"No, Amber. Good grief—you're seven."

Her eyes wilted. Man, these kids were brittle.

"You're a big girl," I said, a little more gently. "Big girls like us sit in our seats."

She immediately sat up straight as if I'd said "Big girls like us face the firing squad without crying."

Tad returned two minutes into the film and crawled around on the floor, trying to mop up a lake of soda.

"What's going on?" he asked when he was finally in his seat again.

I could have told him. I'd already seen the movie. But I just said, "Shhh! Watch and you'll find out."

"Sammie, I'm sleepy," Amber whispered loudly.

"Take a nap," I said.

Tad tugged at my sleeve. "Thanks for bringing me, Sammie. This movie's cool."

I watched him for a few minutes. He gazed at the screen, mouth hanging partially open, lips soundlessly repeating some of the words. Occasionally he'd burst into an explosion of snorts and guffaws, and then he'd stare again, struggling happily to follow the plot.

He was having a wonderful time. But there was something sad about it.

"Finally," Heidi said when the lights came up.

I grabbed her by the arm and said, "Come on, guys," over my shoulder, where Tad was still clapping.

"Sammie?" he said when we got outside.

"Rats!" I said to Heidi.

It was starting to snow, and we had to walk home.

"Sammie?" Tad said again.

"What?" I snapped. "I spent the whole afternoon with you. What do you want now?"

He cowered, but he said again, "Sammie?"

"What is it?"

"Where's Amber?"

I rolled my eyes. "She's right here. She—"

But Amber wasn't behind him, as I'd thought she was, and a quick look around the empty sidewalk showed she wasn't outside at all.

"Maybe she went to the bathroom," Heidi said.

"Right—she'll barely go by herself at home," I said. But I headed for the door anyway.

An overly conscientious usher asked for my ticket. Even when I explained what I was doing, he kept Heidi as collateral while Tad and I dashed in.

Amber wasn't in the bathroom. I tried to keep my heart from pounding right up out of my throat as I hauled Tad by the arm at light speed down the hall to our theatre.

"Did she follow you out?" I said.

He raked his chubby fingers through his hair, his eyes darting like pinballs.

"I don't know—I don't think so—you said come on, so I did." His voice wound up. "I'm stupid. Now my mom and dad won't have anything!"

I stopped dead and turned him to face me.

"What are you talking about?" I said.

"My mom said—" he choked and started to cry.

"What did your mom say, Tad? Come on, it's OK—tell me."

He sobbed loudly and pumped his arms up and down.

"She said my dad got fired 'cause he drank too much beer and it cost a lot for him to go to that hospital and now all they got is us. He's being good and not drinking, and I have to be good, too, because me and Amber's all they got. But I wasn't good, and now she's gone!"

His voice rose to a howl, and I pushed his face up against me and held him there.

"She's not gone," I said, fighting back my own tears. "We'll find her."

He stumbled beside me as I took his big paw and ran with him to the theatre. Another hyper-responsible usher met us inside with his litter scooper in hand, but I shot past him and went for our row.

"We're not letting anybody in yet—"

"Did you find a little girl?" I said, still running.

"There's nobody in here."

But I refused to believe that. I was praying, and hard, when I got to our row. All the seats were empty.

My chest caved in. My parents had asked me to give up one afternoon of my life for my own cousins, who were living a nightmare I couldn't even begin to imagine, and I'd blown it. Worse than blown it—God, please—

"Maybe she's still under the seat," Tad said.

I stared at him, blinking furiously at my tears. "What?"

"When you told her to take a nap she got under the seat. She used to sleep under her bed at home sometimes so she wouldn't hear the yelling."

His words went through me like a switchblade. Hardly daring to breathe, I fumbled down the row and whipped down to look under the chair.

There was Amber, curled up in a ball, sound asleep.

"She's here!" I screamed. "Tad—she's here!"

Tad whooped and Amber sent up a sleepy wail, and I kept saying, "It's all right, you guys!" Even Super Usher got in there, telling us we had to leave as he followed us up the aisle to the door.

Out in the hall, I squashed Amber onto one hip and clung to Tad on the other side. Both of them had their faces buried in my coat, and all three of us were openly bawling. I guess people stared at us as they gathered for the five o'clock show, but I didn't care.

I will personally make sure that these kids have the best Christmas they've ever had, I told God.

Amber nuzzled her snot-covered face in my neck, and I sobbed out loud.

And please, please, I added, *please take care of this pathetic little family.*

"Can we go play in your room now, Sammie?" Tad said.

"Of course," I said, nose running. "What else?"

Color Blind

My first day at Davis, I ran into a trash can and two kids.

The girl looked me up and down, obviously noting that while she was in fashionable knit pants from the Gap, I was in Wal-Mart jeans and a T-shirt.

"Peace on the Planet," she read out loud from my shirt.

The guy tapped the trash can as he pulled her away. "Watch out," he said, "they plant these at regular intervals."

"Peace on the Planet," she said to him again. "Which planet?"

Good question. A sophomore at Jefferson Davis High School in Jacksonville, Florida, my first public school, two thousand miles from any place I'd ever lived, I was wondering which planet I was on. I wasn't blossoming yet, the way Dad had predicted.

"Best public school in the nation," he'd told my sister Katie and me when we'd found out we were moving from Winnemucca, Nevada, to his hometown. "You girls will blossom there."

"It's probably some kind of convent," Katie said to me later.

"Otherwise we'd be in another private school."

In the four places we'd lived since I started first grade, my parents had always sent us to Christian schools. I was waiting for the blossoming to start any time, though I was pretty sure my seeds were still in shock.

But two things happened that first week that shook me out of dormancy.

Shane Chamberlain.

And William Rice.

Coach Doyle pulled me out of P.E. class the day of our fitness tests and said, "Darlin', where did you learn to run like that? I want you on the cross-country team today."

He put his hand on my shoulder as if to keep me from stuttering my head off onto the ground. "I'll give you a private coach to polish up those raw edges."

Dad, of course, was beside himself. "You see!" he said that night. He nudged my mother. "You have room on a shelf for her trophies?"

"Da-ad!"

But he'd grabbed my arm and was pulling me off the couch. "We've got to get to the mall and get you some decent running shoes."

Actually, on the parental scale, my folks rated a ten. If it weren't for their being so disgustingly positive, I'd probably have just crawled into my locker.

The next day I sat on the bleachers, painfully obvious in my new Nikes and running outfit. I was checking for price tags when someone said, "You're safe here. They don't put trash cans on the cross-country route."

My savior from near-death-by-collision-with-a-trash-receptacle dimpled down at me.

"Gonna run cross country?" he said.

I nodded stupidly.

"Saw you run in P.E. You're good."

I nodded again.

"Nice talking to you," he said, grinning.

"I'm just—"

"Here comes Coach with his favorite pet. I'm Shane Chamberlain. You already booked up for the weekend?"

"The weekend?"

"Those two days that come after Friday?"

"Booked up?"

"Do – you – already – have – a – date?"

"Oh. No."

"Keep me in mind."

I didn't tell him, but I didn't think I dated yet. It had never come up.

As soon as Coach Doyle and a guy Shane referred to as his "pet" got within earshot, Shane said, "Hope you're not color blind," and took off.

"William," Coach said, "this is Jill Dority. Diamond in the rough."

William smiled at me. I, in turn, gaped at the steel bands he seemed to have for leg muscles.

"William's our best runner," Coach told me. "You'll be at the front of the pack by the first meet."

As Coach trotted off, yelling something like, "Shane! You jokers hit the track for warm-up," I took another look at William and noticed he had a Tom Cruise smile and deep-set runner's eyes. I don't know when it actually registered that he was black.

"Do you—like—have time—I mean, to be working with me?" I said.

"Training you is training for me," he said. "I'll show you our stretching exercises."

Somewhere in the middle of a set of lunges that had my thigh muscles screaming for mercy, William said, "Did you run track in Nevada?"

"I ran. Not track." He nodded. "There isn't a whole lot to do in Winnemucca, so I used to go jogging in the mountains."

"You have incredible stamina," William said. "You'll mop up the trail with those other girls."

By the end of the first session, I thought I was ready to take on the Boston Marathon.

"You should be a coach," I said.

"Nope. I'm going into law, like my dad. He and I have got to prove that all lawyers aren't crooks. I've gotten early acceptance at Duke for next year. Now all I need is the scholarship money. And hopefully track will do that for me."

"Wow," I said.

"My friend," he said, "you were awesome today."

That's how William Rice became my first official friend at Jeff Davis.

Katie—Kaetea, as she was now suddenly spelling it—had moved a little faster. She was already eating lunch every day with the most popular group in school, which just happened to include Shane's sister.

"Shane really likes you," Katie told me on the way to church one Sunday. "Liz told me so."

"Yeah?" I wasn't sure I was ready to believe that.

"Yeah. If you would just start hanging with him instead of that black guy, he'd be all yours."

"'That black guy' is my friend. Does Liz have a problem with William?"

Katie rolled her eyes. "I don't know. She said her dad says that you can't trust them. Liz just thinks they'll hurt your social standing if you get too close. Know what I mean?"

"I guess." I didn't, but it was enough to plant a seed of doubt inside of me.

The seed was buried by Saturday. It was only a week before our first meet, and William had asked if we could run together over the weekend to step up my training. I'd told him yes. I'd told Shane no. It wasn't that I didn't want to go out. I timed dressing out every day so Shane would catch up with me at the bleachers and flirt shamelessly and make me feel like a girl. But it was like William told me about running: I had to pace myself.

I didn't mention to my parents that William was black. I honestly didn't think it mattered. And there was still that little seed.

The entire Dority family was conveniently in our living room when William's VW pulled up. I had nice visions of Dad slapping him on the back and Mom hovering with a pitcher of iced tea.

But they popped like so many soap bubbles when William got out of the car.

"Oh," Mom said.

Dad didn't say anything.

Once William got to the front porch, Dad met him and stuck out a stiff arm. "Nice to meet you," he said.

No slap on the back. Just a halting voice searching for the polite words.

There wasn't the ghost of an iced tea pitcher.

"You didn't tell him I was black, did you?" William said when they'd retired to the back deck. His face was pinched.

"I didn't think it mattered."

He smiled dully. "Evidently it does."

The seed had now grown into a patch of weeds, but I still had the best five-mile run of my life. En route, when I could gasp, we talked.

I was in awe of everything about him, and I didn't think I had much to contribute to the conversation. But when I found out William had never been beyond Pensacola, I let him pump me for information about the places I'd lived.

"You've been totally nice to me since I moved here," I said when we were cooling down.

"You're 'totally' easy to be nice to," he said. He bent his arm at the elbow. I stared at it stupidly.

"Handshake, girl," he said.

I took his hand and squeezed hard. Sure felt like any other hand.

But as his VW disappeared down the street, the inner weeds got out of control again. Uneasily, I wandered into the back-yard. My parents were still on the deck.

"Have a good run?" Dad asked.

"Yeah," I said.

"I know they can be fantastic runners."

"Who do you mean by 'they'?" I asked.

"Black folks. Some of the greatest runners have been black."

"Because they're black?" I asked.

Mom cleared her throat. "Honey, have you made—other friends?"

"A boy asked me out," I said. And then I added, "He's white."

"How sweet!" she said, relief bubbling from every pore.

"If you want to go out with this fella with a group, it's fine with us, I think," Dad said.

My mother nodded happily. "You're going to be so much more comfortable with—the kind of kids you're used to."

Shane didn't quite fall into that category, but because I didn't know what else to say I mumbled, "OK."

The next week the pressure was on—from William to shorten my running time and from Shane to make a date. I lopped off a whole minute for William. For Shane I squeezed out a "maybe after the meet Saturday" and agreed to run an extra mile just with him after practice on Wednesday.

By then butterflies were having a field day in my stomach. "What's on your mind?" William said.

"I have kind of a date today. With Shane."

"Oh." His face pinched.

"You don't like him?" I said.

"I don't like his ethics."

Shane was in top flirting form that afternoon. I spent more time dodging the arm that kept flying around my shoulder than I did concentrating on my stride. Finally I suggested we walk, but I kept talking.

"Do you embezzle money?" I said.

Shane contorted his face. "Say what?"

"Somebody said you … had different ethics."

"Somebody like William Rice, Counsel for the Prosecution?"

"Maybe."

"Let me tell you something about 'ethics' around here. You

play slave boy to Coach, make him look good, and you get anything you want—including scholarships to fancy schools. Rice has the advantage. Running and being a slave come naturally to him."

"Why?" I asked. But I already knew. I was getting used to it.

"The rest of us have to work our tails off to get noticed," Shane went on. Before I could block, he had his arm around me. "That's why we need beautiful women to take our minds off things."

His contorted face relaxed into a charming smile. I was one of the beautiful, for the first time ever. I hate to admit it, but for the moment I let what he said about William slide.

There were a lot of people at the meet Saturday, including a group of girls holding up a banner reading, "Go For It, Shane!" But Shane assured me it was still "You-and-me, Baby" for the party after the meet.

He gave me a smile, and I was glad I'd let Katie talk me into wearing blush for the race. Still, it was William I really wanted to see.

He was deep in concentration, away from the rest of the team, but when he saw me he grinned.

"Ready?" he said.

"Yeah."

"Psyched up?"

"Yeah."

"Scared spitless?"

"Yeah."

He put up his hand. This time I knew what to do.

"Good luck on your race, too," I said. "You'll get that scholarship."

"Come watch," he said. "After the girls' race, hike out to that stand of trees and see us at the halfway point."

The girls' race was first. I didn't talk to Shane again before we started. He was consulting with his fans. I was too busy concentrating anyway.

It paid off. I came in second. And it was probably the biggest rush I'd ever felt. Dad was at the finish line, pouring water over me.

"That's my girl!" he kept shouting. It was like an incredible dream—until I said, "Daddy, quit! I've got to watch William's race!"

Then I woke up.

"Jill—you remember what your mother and I told you," he said.

"What?"

"About picking your friends."

"Yeah," I said woodenly. "I remember."

For the first time ever I walked away from my father, the weeds growing thistles inside me.

I got to the stand of trees several minutes before the pack rounded the curve. There was no one else there. I climbed a tree so I wouldn't distract them.

It didn't surprise me that William was first to round the curve, but I was startled to see Shane on his heels, with the rest of the pack nowhere in sight. William was moving like a well-oiled machine, eyes straight ahead.

But Shane's eyes were focused on William's feet, and almost before I could wonder why, the toe of Shane's Reebok hooked the back of William's heel. William's ankle jerked, and he dropped like a bag of oranges to the ground.

"Careful!" Shane shouted. He neatly sidestepped William and took off.

For a frozen moment, I stayed plastered to the bark. By the time I scrambled down, William had gotten up and limped on, only steps in front of the pack that rounded the curve.

I'd witnessed a crime—a real crime against the most honest, hardest-working guy I'd ever known. Yet even as I climbed down from the tree, I wasn't sure what I was going to do.

Two things clinched my decision when I got to the finish line.

One was William on the ground, face squeezed shut in pain as Coach Doyle wrapped his ankle.

"What happened?" I heard Coach ask.

"I don't know," William said.

"This ankle's a mess."

The other was my father, slapping Shane on the back, obviously congratulating him on his first place. I marched straight for them.

"Shane!" called his cheering section. "Over here!"

Shane went for them, waving his towel in triumph.

"What happened to the Star?" Dad said to me.

"Why is it," I said, teeth clenched, "that when I make friends with a practically perfect guy who has everything together, you treat him like he doesn't count because he's black? But when I make friends with a chauvinistic, two-faced cheat who had to win a race by tripping somebody on his own team, that's OK because he's white? You didn't even ask if he was a Christian. Why is that, Daddy?"

But I didn't wait for an answer. I ran to the locker room. The thorns were tearing me apart.

I was ready for the lecture and the grounding when I came out dressed, but I didn't care. All I knew was that I was the only one who knew what Shane had done, and I was going to be all alone in telling.

Dad was waiting outside. "Your mother took the car. I told her we'd walk."

He shoved his hands into his pockets, and I realized he was miserable too.

"I've been away from racial tension for a long time," he said. "The only black people I've even seen for the past ten years were on *The Cosby Show.* I thought all the beliefs that were drummed into me when I was a boy were gone."

"What beliefs?" I asked.

"That black people can run and tap dance and not much else. That their families are always poor and uneducated." He looked at me sheepishly. "That nice white girls don't associate with black boys. But now I've come to the awful realization that once you're back in the old situation, the old beliefs are still there, and you've got to chop them up with a garden hoe."

"Then you *are* prejudiced," I said.

"I am. But I don't want to be. I want to be like you—taking everybody for the person they are."

I looked at him in surprise. "You're the one who taught me that," I said.

"Now it's your turn to teach me."

I started to cry then, and he put his arm around me.

My words came out in torrents. "Shane cheated, and he's ruined something that's really important to William—and I'm the only one who knows about it. I have to tell on him."

"Yes, you do."

"Will you help me?"

"I'm behind you all the way."

I sagged against his ten-rated shoulder. "Thanks, Dad."

I knew he *would* be behind me all the way. And that was exactly what I needed.

Jesse's Girl

"Megs, this thing with Jesse has gotten out of hand. You've got to stop it."

"'Hi, Meg, how are you?'" Meg said dryly from the spot in front of the TV where she was painting her toenails. "Oh, fine, Lucie, and yourself?"

"Knock it off. Now come on, we have to talk." Lucie took the family room in two strides and switched off the television.

"Hey! That was *Days of Our Lives!*"

"Big deal. Meg—talk to me."

"About what?" Meg twisted the cap onto the bottle of nail polish, stubbornly avoiding Lucie's green eyes.

"You and Jesse. What happened?"

"It doesn't matter."

"Then why have you been acting like somebody died ever since Saturday night? And don't deny it. Everybody in youth group has noticed it."

"It isn't 'everybody in youth group's' business," Meg said, without taking her own brown eyes off her wet toenails.

"It is too! You two not speaking to each other makes it just a little uncomfortable for the rest of us, y'know what I'm saying? Me-eg!" Lucie snatched the polish bottle from her. "You and Jesse have been friends—forever! It just seems real weird that suddenly you hate each other. And since we're all practically family, it makes everybody feel crummy. Come on," she said, her voice softening. "Just tell me what he did, or what you did—or whatever."

Meg wordlessly pulled a strip of her hair under her nose.

Lucie stood up in exasperation. "OK. Fine. Be that way."

"There's no other 'way' to be. I thought Jesse cared about me; he evidently doesn't. In fact, he is evidently a creep—and I'm mad about it. I have a right to be mad."

"OK, so he did something to hurt your feelings." Lucie poked her hands onto her hips. "What about 'turning the other cheek'?"

Meg raked her fingers through her hair. "Why? So he can smack the other one, too?" She dropped her hands into her lap. "Sorry. This is one cheek that isn't going to turn."

Lucie looked at her for a long minute before angrily snapping the TV on. "All right. But don't forget what you owe the rest of us, OK? Like the carnival committee meeting tomorrow after school. Think you can stomach seeing Jesse there?"

Meg nodded glumly.

When Lucie was gone, Meg shut off *Days of Our Lives* with a wet-nailed toe. She wished it were as easy to turn off the scenes that kept running through her mind.

It would have been bad enough if it were just Saturday night that was on constant replay. But the good times—those were the memories that hurt the most right now.

She rolled over, slid a *People* magazine off the coffee table and flipped aimlessly through it. She and Jesse seemed to be on every page.

Scooting around in his old orange Volkswagen with the top down, the tape deck blaring, and the two of them sucking up Slurpees as if 7-Eleven were going out of business tomorrow.

Lying on their stomachs at Mills Park, pulling the petals out of dandelions and comparing dreams. And Jesse not even being ashamed to cry in front of her when the dreams became too much.

Sitting together in church; poking each other whenever old Mr. Newhouse nodded off in the pew in front of them; glancing at each other whenever Rev. Todd said something that hit home.

Just looking at Jesse, with his rusty-colored hair, his blue eyes that other people said were too close together, and his lumberjack shoulders—the ones he'd taken her piggyback on across the school parking lot when they were late coming back from lunch—before they had run smack into Mr. Rodriguez, Dean of Boys.

She'd stolen those looks only when Jesse couldn't see, because for Jesse their relationship was strictly a friendship. Buddies. Sister and brother. And although Meg would have loved to have had it otherwise, she'd decided sixteen months ago, when they'd first started weaving their strange and wonderful relationship together, that that could be enough for her.

Meg slapped the magazine closed. It was time to get up and do something—anything—before the rerun of what had happened Saturday night went on in her brain again.

She was able to keep her mental television off until the carnival committee meeting the next afternoon. Then nothing could keep the pain from coming into view.

Just being in the youth group room brought back images of her and Jesse tearing all over the church, trying to get members of the congregation to volunteer to be dunked in their booth at the community churches' fall carnival.

Seeing Jesse at the meeting made it worse. Seeing that Cary was with him made it unbearable.

I guess it worked, Jesse, she thought bitterly when they walked in, because here she is, falling all over you.

Cary saw her and glanced quickly away. Jesse didn't look at her at all.

"OK, guys, we gotta get a move on," Lucie said. "I've got my dad's pick-up outside and it's loaded up with wood—compliments of Jesse's dad."

Jesse took an exaggerated bow amid equally exaggerated applause from the group. Meg rolled her eyes.

That's it. Show off, she thought. *It's what you do best.* Ugliness clawed at her throat.

It took the six kids three hours and two trips to 7-Eleven to get the dunking booth put together. Meg stayed behind both times. She couldn't stand to even look at a Slurpee.

When they came back from the second run, Jesse and Cary were in the back of the truck. As they pulled up, Jesse vaulted his long body over the side and put his arms up to lift Cary out. Meg felt a rising wave of nausea.

"Cut the hanky panky, Matthews," Thad Rhoades called to Jesse. "We've still got work to do."

"Eat your heart out," Jesse said, grinning his crooked grin.

"Don't have to. With a face like mine, I have to beat the women away with a stick."

Jesse snorted. "With a face like yours …"

"At least his eyes aren't too close together."

Five incredulous stares turned on Meg, whose gaze hooked

up with Jesse's for only a moment before she turned away and brought a panel of hair under her nose.

"Real nice, Meg," Geoff muttered.

"Really!" That came from Lucie, who was looking hard at her.

"I think your eyes are great," Cary said.

Meg whirled around again. "Yeah, Jesse, don't cry," she retorted. "She thinks your eyes are great."

This time no one looked at Meg.

Her mental prediction that Lucie would call her the minute she got home was right.

"Meg, what is your problem?" she asked in lieu of hello.

"I don't have a problem," Meg snapped. But she knew she sounded even less convincing than she felt.

"If you were just naturally a snake, it wouldn't have blown everybody away when you said those things to Jesse. But you're not like that. What is *wrong?*"

The ugliness climbed up Meg's throat again and spilled over.

"I hate myself, Luce," she admitted tearfully. "But I hate him more. I can't stand this. I'm thinking of dropping out of youth group."

"I'm coming over."

Lucie was sitting on the other end of Meg's bed almost before she'd hung up.

"I'm not leaving until you tell me what happened," she said. "Spill it."

Meg did. In bits and pieces ripped torturously out of her memory, she got the story out.

It had started the Monday before, she told Lucie, when Jesse had mentioned how cute he thought Cary Baker was. It hadn't bothered Meg, exactly, because Jesse always gave her his impressions of other girls. He dated around. She'd even helped him finagle an introduction or two. After all, he and Meg were just friends.

But there had been something different about the way he reacted to Cary—or maybe it was the way Cary reacted to him. He had never mentioned her again to Meg, but she had noticed that Jesse sought out opportunities to talk to Cary and when they arose, Cary gave a saccharin smile, (Sweet 'n' Low Smirk, Lucie called it), tossed her blonde mane, and moved on.

It had been an open and shut case of playing hard to get as far as Meg was concerned. Although she'd been tempted to point out to Jesse that Cary was a snob, he had made it plain he didn't want to discuss it.

He'd been so distracted all week, Meg had been freaked out when he suddenly called around six Saturday afternoon and suggested they go down to Pizza Hut. "A bunch of kids" were going to be there, he said, and it might be fun.

It had been anything but fun, right from the start. Jesse had been quiet and had even turned up the volume on the car radio while Meg was in the middle of a sentence.

At Pizza Hut they had sat with a crowd of kids neither Meg nor Jesse knew very well, and Jesse had kept such close surveillance on the parking lot, he didn't even talk to Meg.

Then, abruptly, he'd grabbed her by the arm and practically lifted her out of the chair.

"Let's go outside," he'd said huskily.

"We haven't even eaten yet. I'm starved!"

"It'll wait. Come on."

He'd locked his arm around her waist and propelled her out

the front door before she could even grab her jacket.

"Jesse, it is freezing out here," she'd said when the November wind hit her.

"Don't worry, Baby," he'd said in a voice too loud for Jesse. "I'll keep you warm."

Then he'd pulled her up tight against him—and tried to kiss her.

"At first I couldn't believe it," Meg said, looking up from her bedspread at Lucie. "I mean, even though I'd accepted that we were strictly on the buddy system, I always really did want it to be—different."

"So, was it?"

"It wasn't what I expected. I dreamed of him kissing me enough times, believe me, and I always thought he would be tender and gentle. But he wasn't. It was like he didn't even care how I felt. He just grabbed me and tried to lay one on me. I wasn't ready for that, so I turned away."

"But I don't get it. If your relationship changed that night—"

"It didn't—not that way." Meg churned miserably against the pillows.

"Keep going."

"I hate this part."

"It's OK to cry," Lucie said softly.

So Meg did, as she talked.

When she'd turned back toward Jesse, she'd expected to see him looking down at her with the same mixture of wonder and confusion she'd felt tumbling inside of her. But though his arms were still around her, his eyes had been staring above her head. Meg had pulled away and followed his gaze—right to Cary, who was standing at the entrance, looking back at Jesse

Matthews, Casanova, with new interest.

"From that moment on, I've hated him," Meg said, swiping at the two streams on her cheeks.

"You don't hate him …"

"He used me. He was my best friend. We trusted each other." Meg's voice was rising dangerously, and she drew in a deep breath. "The thing is, he didn't have to do that to me. I'd have helped him get Cary if that's what he wanted—and he knew it."

Lucie looked at her helplessly. "I know, Megs, but this jealousy is doing a real number on you."

"It's more than jealousy. He hurt me—bad."

"Does he know that?"

Meg rolled her eyes. "He isn't stupid."

"Maybe he is, because he was asking us when we went to get hamburgers today if anybody knew why you still weren't speaking to him."

Meg straightened her shoulders. "Then maybe somebody ought to tell him."

"Somebody like me?"

"No," Meg said. "Somebody like me."

Finding Jesse alone, without Cary, wasn't easy. In only a week they'd become Siamese twins. It wasn't until late Saturday afternoon, when the carnival was almost over, that the opportunity presented itself. Oddly enough, it was Jesse who made the first move.

Meg was counting money when he was suddenly at her elbow.

"How did we do?" he said.

Meg stiffened. "About a hundred dollars."

"All right! The Methodists only made fifty-six at the hotdog stand. Hey, did you see me dunk Mr. Rodriguez? Got him back for that time he caught us …"

He stopped. Meg's eyes were switchblades.

"What's wrong?" he said. His voice was barely audible, so different from the raucous one that had said, "Don't worry, Baby. I'll keep you warm."

"You don't even know, do you?" Meg said. "You're just going on and on about money and the Methodists and old times. You …" She slammed the lid to the money box and angrily yanked her hair behind her ears. "I really thought we were good friends—and then you used me."

Jesse's face contorted into a question mark. "I thought you'd understand. You always understand me—at least you used to."

Meg wanted to grab the front of his jacket and shake him. Instead, she jabbed her hands into the pockets of her jeans and pulled herself up as far as she could.

"You asked too much of me that time, Jesse. You hurt me."

As she stood there, straining to keep her head high, Jesse's bigness seemed to crumple. His shoulders sagged, and Meg saw him swallow hard.

"I really didn't know, Meg," he said finally.

She looked at the ground. "Well, now you do."

There was a long, sad silence. Jesse reached out to lift her chin, but she pulled away. He looked stung.

"Maybe you won't believe this," he said, "but I'm sorry. I really am sorry."

Then he walked away.

Incredibly, the earth kept turning. The rest of the money somehow got counted. Geoff and Thad dunked Lucie before they took down the booth, and everyone finally drifted off toward the bonfire. Meg decided not to stay, but she wandered close to it for a minute to try to stop the uncontrollable shivering that had suddenly taken hold of her.

All the youth groups were there, gathered in knots against the late fall chill to celebrate another successful carnival. Jesse was there, too. Meg spotted him right away, just a few steps down from her. The shadows and flames were flickering across his face, playing tricks on it—making it look at one moment like the young Jesse she'd loved so much, at the next like an older, wiser Jesse she would probably never know now.

That was sad. But she realized, in the flash of one flame, that she didn't hate him anymore. She didn't like him. She didn't want him touching her on the chin or assuming they were friends. But at least she didn't hate him.

She turned away from the blaze and started home, the pumpkin-frost air at once taking the fire out of her face.

Why? She wondered. Maybe it was because he'd said he was sorry.

Sorry. It hadn't occurred to her that she should forgive him. Maybe that was what Lucie meant by "turn the other cheek"—not just so he could let fly with another punch, but so he'd have another chance not to.

She pulled her jacket tight across her chest. *I can't*, she thought, the tears starting to come. *It hurts too much.*

But, "I'm really sorry." He had said that, and he had looked like he meant it.

Meg stopped and turned back to look at the bonfire.

What was the point in youth groups and church carnivals and all the friendships that came out of them if you forgot that God was the reason for it all? It was a cinch He wasn't just there for the dunking booth.

She glanced around. The street was empty, so she said it out loud.

"I can't forgive him—yet," she said. "But—I'm sorry, too."

Wiping the tears off her cheeks with the sleeve of her jacket, she again started toward home. Tomorrow she'd have to tell Lucie—maybe the cheek was starting to turn, after all.

It Must Be
So Easy
Being
a Guy

Swimming in the Shallow End

Yeah, the blue outfit's fine," I said into the phone. "You look good in that."

"I don't want to look 'good,' Andy," Kathryn said. "I want to look fabulous."

"OK, you look fabulous in it. What time do you want to go?"

"You don't think it makes me look fat?" she said.

"You couldn't look fat if you wore inflatable jeans. Gumby weighs more than you do."

"I don't want to look like Gumby!"

"I didn't say you looked like Gumby …"

Across the room Nathan rolled his eyes.

"Kath," I said, "you'd be incredible if you wore a Macy's bag, OK? I'm gonna have to fight off every guy at WinterFaire."

Nathan stuck his finger down his throat.

"You're so sweet," Kathryn said.

I told her I'd pick her up at four o'clock and then got off the phone.

"What was that all about?" Nathan said.

"We're going to that WinterFaire carnival they've got going downtown tomorrow," I said. "We're gonna do the whole shoot-wooden-ducks-for-teddy-bears-eat-cotton-candy thing."

"No, I'm talking about the whole oh-Andy-tell-me-I-look-like-Cindy-Crawford thing," Nathan said.

"You're hallucinating," I said.

"Bet me." Nathan made a stupid voice. "'You'd be incredible in a Macy's bag.'" He groaned. "You're messed up, man."

I didn't say anything. I don't normally. I've always been more of a listener, and Nathan had me intrigued.

"She's got you trained," he said. "You told her three times she looked terrific, and she was still whining for more. If she were my girlfriend, she and I would have a talk."

"About what?"

"About she goes her way, I go mine," Nathan said.

"Why?"

"Shallow. She's about as deep as a puddle."

There was a tap on the door—my mom telling us our pizza had arrived.

And that, of course, was the end of the conversation, Nathan being the "deep" type.

Besides, he didn't know Kathryn.

I'd never noticed her before I saw "Grease" at school. The girl could sing—LeAnn Rimes, eat your heart out. When everybody took their bows at the end, I was surprised at how many other people were in the show. I'd been looking at her the whole time.

I checked her name in the program—Kathryn Gates—but I totally ruled her out as a possible date. Not that she didn't blow me away with her petite figure, blond hair, enormous blue eyes, and smile that lit up the stage. I just figured she was way out of my league.

Until one of the ushers invited me to the cast party.

"I know how you are about drinking and stuff, Andy," she said, with innocent eyes. "It's all gonna be soda and chips."

So what's the first thing I saw when I got there? The stage manager shoving a Budweiser in Kathryn Gates' face.

"I don't drink," she was telling him. She was trying to be cool about it, but her huge blue eyes were darting everywhere like she was scared to death.

"I bet you've never even tried it," the guy said.

"She says she doesn't want to," I said. "Why don't you back off?"

"What are you doing here?" Mr. Budweiser asked. "You're not in the cast."

"I'm not here," I said. "I'm gone."

I didn't even get off the front porch before Kathryn was out the door after me.

When I dropped her off at her house about two hours later, I felt like she'd shot me full of adrenaline.

I had found out she was not only good looking, but she was a Christian like me. She felt the same way I did about a lot of things: drinking, sex, stuff like that. Since the cast party two months ago, she'd been giving my life a kick it hadn't had before.

It was weird, though. Lately, I felt as if I was the one doling out the energy. Even right now, after a ten-minute conversation, I felt more tired than I did after two hours of basketball.

I hadn't focused on it until tonight, but maybe Nathan was right. Maybe Kathryn did depend too much on me telling her that she was drop-dead gorgeous.

No big deal, I decided. I'd just quit reassuring her every ten seconds. End of problem.

At first it didn't look like it was going to be that hard. She slid into the front seat when I picked her up the next afternoon and instead of saying, "Does my hair look stupid like this?" she asked, "Did you get your schedule in the mail today?"

"Yeah," I said. "I can't believe we only have two days of Christmas break left. Who'd you get for English?"

"Toti, first hour," she said. "Then math, environmental science, computer typing fourth, study hall, history. And I got Caxton for that—everybody says he's easy."

"When do you have chorus?" I asked.

"I'm not taking it this semester."

I took my eyes off the road long enough to stare at her.

"Why not?" I said. "Chorus is your big thing!"

"I don't need it," she said. "I'm gonna be way too busy."

"Doing what?"

"Going to your basketball games. If I'm in chorus, I'll have to miss half of them because of rehearsals. Besides, you might need me to help you study. You have to keep your grades up to get a scholarship. You said that."

"What about *your* grades?" I said.

"I don't need a 4.0."

I didn't answer. This conversation was turning lame. I was tired already, and I wasn't even pumping her up.

But things looked up when we got to the Faire. How can you feel tired when you're surrounded by eight-foot-tall snowmen coaxing you to ice skate and barkers luring you to win big, stuffed Tweety Birds? Especially when your girlfriend looks like a shiny-eyed little girl smiling at you over her blue cotton candy.

I was jazzed again, and I got Kathryn into the ice palace, got her on the Eskimo slide, and even took her on a carriage ride where we had to bundle up in a blanket to keep warm. She laughed her song of a laugh and cuddled up next to me. I thought about Nathan being enough of a jerk to give this up just because he didn't understand women.

Then we walked past a guy who shouted, "IF I CAN'T GUESS YOUR WEIGHT WITHIN TWO POUNDS, YOU WIN A FREE PRIZE!"

"Forget that," Kathryn groaned. "I'm not telling my weight in front of anybody!"

"Knock that off, Kath," I said, a little harshly. "Half the girls at school would kill to look like you, and you know it."

Her eyes immediately swam with tears. You'd have thought I'd slapped her. I felt like some kind of brute.

"I'm going to the bathroom," she said, voice quavery. "I'll be right back."

I was glad for the break. Man, she was even more sensitive than I had thought.

Or was it sensitive? What had Nathan called her? Shallow?

I'd told myself to be afraid if I ever started taking advice from Nathan, but it was almost as if he had a point this time. Was that really all Kathryn cared about—looking perfect, making sure every eyelash was in place?

She came out of the bathroom then, lips all slick and hair braided. She'd apparently decided not to cry. She put her hand in mine, tilted her chin up, and said, "Let's walk on the boulevard."

"Whatever," I said.

I felt less like talking than ever. As we dodged the old guys pushing even older couples bundled into rickshaws and the hordes of people shoving their way into coffee shops, I looked around for something to do.

I scanned past the boulevard, and my eyes lit on a good possibility.

"Come on," I said. "Let's go do that."

"What?" Kathryn asked. Her face brightened like she was glad I'd said something—anything.

"Karaoke," I said.

Kathryn giggled as I dragged her across the street. "You're gonna sing?"

"No," I said. "You are."

It was ten bucks a song, and you got to keep the tape.

"Andy, no!" Kathryn said as I forked over the money. "I'll be embarrassed!"

"Why?" I asked. "You have a great voice."

Man, I was doing it again. It was like she was manipulating me into giving her compliments. I gave her a little shove.

"Pick a song," I said.

She actually looked a little freaked-out as she blinked at the selection of songs.

"Do something by Celine Dion," I said. "What about 'Because You Love Me'? Do that."

At that point I think she'd have done Pearl Jam if I'd suggested it. She looked like she was slipping into shock.

The guy got her set up with a microphone and a TV screen showing the lyrics. She stared at both of them as if they were gonna whip out fangs and bite her.

"What's the big deal?" I said. "Just sing."

The music started, and then the letters on the screen flashed red. Her mouth automatically flew open.

At first her voice sounded like somebody was holding a gun to her head, and I thought, *Give me a break. Enough with the act already.* If I hadn't been so annoyed—and maybe even a bit smug—I would have been disappointed. I had really thought there was more to her.

And then, slowly, she started to sing. Not just sing and sound really good, but sing like she meant it … like she felt it. The song didn't just flow from her—it worked its way out like a deep-felt emotion. It almost hurt to see her sing, yet I couldn't take my eyes off of her.

A crowd had gathered around the booth by the time she finished the song, and everybody clapped. Her blue eyes startled, until she saw me. And then she lit up the boulevard with her smile. She wasn't shallow. She just hadn't discovered her own depth yet. But she had to be seeing it now. There was no way she could miss it.

I grabbed her when she stepped out of the booth, tape in hand.

"That was incredible," I said. "Kath, you can't quit chorus. You have to keep singing."

She laughed and dropped the tape into her purse. "Why?"

"Get away from me with that dog food," I said. "You know why. You love it. It's in you."

"Yeah," she said, "but there are about a million other girls with voices just as good as mine."

It was like I'd handed her a soda and she'd thrown it in my face. I couldn't believe it.

"Would you stop it?" I snapped at her.

Several people turned around and looked at us. I stomped off down the sidewalk to the old courthouse and took the steps three at a time. She caught up to me when I hurled myself down onto the top one.

"What's wrong?" she said.

I gave her a jerky shrug. Inside, I was seething.

"Come on, Andy," she said. "I hate it when you clam up."

That did it. I exploded, right there under the sculpture of Lady Justice.

"The only reason you want me to talk is so you can hear about how wonderful you are every ten seconds," I shouted. "That's all you want!"

Her eyes overflowed, and she didn't try to stop them this time. The hurt twisted her face, and I felt bad about it. But I also felt trapped and squeezed and pushed and tired. I just shoved my hands in my pockets and chewed my cheek.

"I don't *want* you to reassure me, Andy," she said with tears in her throat. "I *need* you to. I just feel ugly and ordinary. I keep thinking that if you tell me enough that I'm pretty and special, I might start to believe it."

Suddenly, it all came together for me. Why being with her was giving me chronic fatigue syndrome. Why one minute I thought she was shallow and the next I thought she was a basket case.

"What?" Kathryn said. There was desperation in her voice. "Talk to me, Andy. Is it the chorus thing? I can still change my schedule."

I looked down at her. Man, she really was gorgeous, and talented, and full of feelings I'd probably never have. She was deeper than me and Nathan put together.

"Would you be doing it for you or for me?" I said.

"I don't care!" she said, her face white-scared. "I just want you to be happy. If it will make you proud of me, then I'll do it …"

I grabbed her by the shoulders. "Kathryn!" I said. "Your self-esteem can't be my responsibility."

"What do you mean?" she said. "I don't get it."

I could have told her. Maybe as a good Christian kid I should have. Except it wouldn't have been enough. Ever. And it still would have been me telling her—not Kathryn exploring the depths of herself.

And I was tired of swimming in the shallow end.

"Come on, Kath," I said. "I'll drive you home."

The Interview

Shaun? Could I talk to you?"

I am Shaun—but so were about 30 percent of the guys in the senior class. I hoped the girl was talking to one of the other ones, and I kept walking.

Make that hobbling, on crutches. The stupid things burnt my armpits, but I cruised on at double speed toward the empty table across the library. The girl followed me.

"Aren't you Shaun Cornell?" she said as I parked my appendages and maneuvered my cast around the table leg so I could sit down.

"Yeah," I said through my teeth.

"I don't think you know me. I'm Taryn Johnson."

I dropped into the chair with a thud and said, "And your point is?"

"I was wondering if I could interview you for *The Minuteman*."

Up to this point I hadn't looked at her. My head jerked up now to see if she was really an escapee from our local mental health institution. *The Minuteman* was our school newspaper.

But she looked pretty much sane as she read my face and said, "A lot of people are bummed about what happened. The staff thought a story on you would answer a lot of questions …"

"I don't want to talk about it," I said.

"I won't pry into your personal life. Just a few facts, what your plans are now—"

"I tore an interior tendon. I've had major reconstructive surgery twice—and I don't have any plans!" I flopped open an encyclopedia that was lying on the table and stared down at it. "There's your article," I said. "Go for it."

"Thanks so much," she said above my head. "You've been great about this."

Out of the corner of my eye, I watched her hurry to one of the computers in the corner. I felt like I'd just slapped her. But hey—I didn't even know the chick—and she *was* prying into my personal life.

"Hey, Shaun." Dan Barber pulled a chair up next to mine and peered into my face. "Dude, is it really true?" he said.

I could feel my jaw muscles contracting.

"What?"

"About you not playing basketball anymore?"

"Yeah."

"No, man, I mean, not like, forever?"

"Yes," I said tightly. I plastered my eyes into the encyclopedia.

"Whoa, dude, that really bites big time. But, I mean, does that mean no college ball?"

"College would be part of forever," Angie Thraikill said dryly from the next table. "What's to wig out over, anyway? It's a game. I don't get what the big deal is."

"Leave him alone," Carly Towers said. She was sitting next to Angie, her cocker spaniel eyes drooping at me. "Can't you see he's messed up about it?"

"And can't any of you see I'm trying to get something done here?" I stood up and sent my crutches clattering to the floor. Half the library froze, and the other half scurried over to grab them.

Ms. Howser sprayed us all with a "shhh" about then and everybody buried their heads back in their term papers. I retrieved my crutches and swung over to the computer in the corner.

"Hey, Tanya," I said.

"Taryn," she said without looking up.

"I'll give you the interview. Maybe it'll get everybody out of my face."

She swiveled around in the chair and looked up at me. It was the first time I noticed how huge—and blue—her eyes were.

Since the next day was Saturday, she came over to my house to do her thing. I was propped up in the family room when my dad sent her in. Her big eyes roamed from the fireplace to the popcorn in the green bowl on the table to the bookshelves that lined the walls.

"Great room," she said. "It feels good in here."

"I think it's hot in here," I said.

She pulled a notebook out of her backpack and looked at me curiously. "First question," she said. "Have you always been this negative, or is it a result of your injury?"

I stared at her. "Negative?" I said.

"Well, yeah. I mean, this is only our second conversation, but all I've heard come out of your mouth is downer stuff, which surprises me. I always heard you were this great guy, in spite of the fact that you're a jock."

"I *was* a jock," I said. "I'm not anymore. Isn't that what you're supposed to be asking me about?"

She pulled a pencil from behind her ear and tapped it on the notebook. "I'm supposed to find out the answers to every-body's questions. So let's start with Angie Thraikill's. 'What's to wig out over? Basketball's just a game, isn't it?'"

"It wasn't to me," I said, and then bit my lip. Maybe this wasn't such a good idea after all.

"Look, Shaun," Taryn said. The softness in her voice made me look up at her. "Why don't you just tell me your story the way you want it printed? What's that going to hurt?"

I shrugged and started talking.

"I've always looked at my whole life like it's a basketball game," I told her. "And I think it's being played in four quar-ters. That would figure, since I've spent the best part of it on a basketball court—and also the worst part.

"The first quarter was about preparation. My dad's the coach at Springfield, you know, the private college. So I had a regula-tion basketball almost before I could carry it. And when I was seven, I got a hoop in the driveway on an adjustable pole. Every time Dad had to raise it to match my height—several times a year in middle school—it was like a ceremony. I spent most of my spare time shooting baskets, dribbling, practicing free throws, guarding my dad. He's 6'2". By the time I was four-teen, I was already 6'3".

"Neither of us could wait for my sophomore year when I could finally put to use all the summers of basketball camps and the nights of playing one-on-one with Dad until 2:00 in the morning.

"I could feel the first quarter coming to an end and the second quarter starting when I looked at the team list in the gym that day in November. It was my sophomore year, and my name was on the varsity list. I was a *starter* my sophomore year—and even though some guys resented me for that at first, the team was winning. We were 25 and 7 that year, and a lot of it was because of me. I was jacking ten rebounds a game, averaging twenty-two, twenty-three points, three or four assists.

"Anyway, that isn't bragging. I knew I was good only because I had a gift from God."

"God?"

I stopped for the first time and looked at Taryn.

"Yeah, God," I said. "See, anybody who knows anything about basketball will tell you there are a lot of good players who get the job done, but most of them tend to be mechanical. Then there are the ones who have a natural gift. It's just different to watch them because they flow. I'm one of those. I can feel it when I play. It's like God takes over and makes it work. I don't know how else to put it."

She nodded. "Go on."

"That doesn't mean I didn't work at it. No matter how good you are, you have to want it—and I did."

"Want what?"

"The Vision."

I stopped again. I hadn't thought about the Vision since after my second operation. Thinking about it just made it hurt more. But now, with Taryn's big eyes staring me down, it started coming out again.

"I planned to get a full scholarship to play ball at one of the major schools—U. Mass. Or Duke or Syracuse—and then go to the Lakers or the Celtics. I know that's the dream of every kid who has ever put on a pair of high tops, but it started to seem more and more real—and not just to me.

"By the end of my sophomore year and on into my junior season, the scouts that came to look at seniors were asking about me. One guy from Wake Forest asked Coach if I'd consider graduating early! They were all saying that it was rare to find a hard-working player who was also gifted.

"What they didn't know was that it's even rarer to find a player who knows where that gift comes from. I wasn't afraid to tell anybody who'd listen that I was blessed by God, that the Lord was always with me on the court. That's why I'm so ticked off. That's what's to wig out over ..."

"You're mad at God, then," Taryn said, still scribbling madly.

"You're dang straight! Junior year, every game I was making four or five steals, jacking sixteen rebounds a game, averaging twenty-seven to twenty-eight points, five or six assists. We're up ten points in the district finals and I'm going for every score I can. I'm outside the paint and this guy's guarding me, so I do a head fake and drive hard to the hole. Here comes a man right at me full-throttle. He doesn't expect me to be there. Bam—he catches me just right—I go down."

In a heap, I didn't add. A screaming, bawling, clawing heap. The pain from my knee brought me down like a baby. Nothing could have kept me from screaming as they carried me off the court.

If I'd known what it was all going to mean, I'd probably have cried harder.

I looked up now. Taryn was chewing on the end of her pencil and flipping back through her notes.

"That was last year—junior year," she said. "But you played this year."

"Yeah, I did. They told me when I blew my knee that first time that even with reconstructive surgery and rehab, one false move on the court and I could blow it again."

Taryn's face crinkled. "But you came back and played anyway."

"Yeah. I didn't think the doctors were figuring God into it. I knew God really wanted me to be a Christian athlete and represent Him on the court and in the locker room, so He wouldn't let that happen to me. I'd beat the odds."

"But you didn't."

"No," I said bitterly. I could feel my face burning. "I didn't. Halfway through the season, my knee blew. It's over. I'll never play ball again."

Taryn had stopped writing. She selected a couple of pieces of popcorn and chewed them thoughtfully before she said, "So basically now—you're angry."

"I think I have a right to be! I was doing what God wanted me to do and now He's taken it all away. So, yeah, I'm ticked. Matter of fact, I don't even know if I believe in Him anymore."

I hadn't shared that thought with anybody, even though it had been shouting in my brain ever since the night I'd been injured. But Taryn didn't look shocked. She just cocked her head and said, "Gee, I wish I could just stop believing my father exists. I'm mad at him all the time."

I looked at her stupidly. "What?" I said.

"How can you be mad at somebody who doesn't exist?"

"You can't, but ..."

She leaned back into the couch and folded her arms. "You want to know something?" she said.

"Do I have a choice?"

"For two years, people have been telling me that God can make everything OK again, and I've laughed up my sleeve because I haven't even believed there could be a God—until today. You are so furious. I mean, He has to be there if you're using up so much energy being mad at Him."

I could feel my lip curling into a sneer. "What are you saying?"

"I'm saying I think God gave you more than a gift for dribbling a ball. I think He gave you the gift to be passionate. Now you just have to shift your passion to something else."

"You know something?" I said through clenched teeth. "I am so sick of people having all the answers for me when they don't even know what it means to never again have something you have loved, that you thought was going to be there forever."

"Really," she said.

Her voice was cold, and her big eyes suddenly matched it. She tossed the notebook and pencil across the table at me. "Take notes, Cornell. I'm going to tell you my story."

I didn't move. She went on anyway.

"My father, bless his heart, is a cocaine addict. All of us tried to help him—he blew us off. Anyway, one night two years ago, he and my mother went out and he got loaded as usual. On the way home, he went the wrong way on an expressway ramp and ran head-on into a Corvette coming the other way.

"The seventeen-year-old girl driving the 'Vette and my mother were both killed. My father's supposedly spending fifteen years in the state prison. Two down, two more to go until he comes up for parole. By then I'll be out of the foster home I'm in and on my own and I won't have to deal with him if I don't want to. So, basically, I lost it all."

If I could have ripped my own lips off, I'd have done it right then. My only other choice was to mumble, "I'm sorry. I'm really sorry."

"Don't be," she said. "Until today all I could do was be angry at my father—so angry I wished he had been the one to die in the accident. I felt so guilty all the time. But now I have somebody else to be mad at. It's a start."

I didn't answer. I wasn't sure it *was* a start—until she looked at me with her big, magic eyes and said, "Maybe we could be mad at Him together."

That was January. Now that it's March and the world's starting to wake up some, I think I am, too.

Taryn and I are getting past our anger, thanks to the loss group at my church that we both joined. Her anger, it turned out, went even deeper than mine. And, of course, she had to get to know God as somebody besides a target for mental spitballs. That's where I came in.

We also went to one basketball game. I thought I'd hate not being down there, driving toward the hole. But I only felt sad, as if I was already far removed from it all. The third quarter was over for me. And that's where Taryn came in.

She says basketball was something I did, not something I was. I like that—even though now I'm in the fourth quarter and I don't know what the game plan is. I'm waiting for God to show me.

Oh, and about the article. It never came out in *The Minuteman*. Taryn never wrote it. It was never an assignment in the first place.

"I was just looking for answers," she admitted to me.

Thank God she had some.

When I Was Benjie

We're still looking at a few hours, Ben," the nurse with the fabulous brown eyes said to me. "Your sister really wants you in there with the family."

"Like I told her," I said, "watching somebody have labor pains doesn't really do anything for me." I smiled at Brown Eyes. "Now, going down to the coffee shop and having a Coke is a whole other thing. You want to join me?"

"I'm on duty," she said. "I'll let you know when the baby's close. You won't want to miss that."

I did want to miss that. That's why I was in the waiting room looking at five-month-old copies of *Newsweek* instead of hovering around my sister Kate's bed in the birthing room, listening to my parents squeal with every contraction.

"That's OK," I said. "Just let me know when you go on a break."

Brown Eyes laughed and left. Girls don't usually laugh when I ask them out. But then, this one was wearing a wedding ring. I'd never asked a married woman out before.

I rifled through the magazines on the table for the fifteenth time and then dug into my jeans pocket for change. I could call somebody. Amy or Julianna or Kiffany. Somebody who didn't want to discuss how wonderful somebody's pain was.

"It is first necessary to dial one," a nasal voice told me when I dialed Amy's number.

Dude. I'd been in this hospital waiting room so long I'd forgotten that I was two towns away from home. Of course, I used to live here in Hudson …

I was so desperately bored, I actually picked up the phone book and started thumbing through it. But after two pages of Jones and Johnson, I let it swing from its chain again. That was fifth grade. Nobody was going to remember me from five years ago. Hopefully.

I bought another pack of Life Savers and collapsed on the couch on top of two dog-eared copies of *People*. It would've been cool if I could've just kicked back at Kate and Gary's. Mom could've called me to tell me whether I had a niece or a nephew. I'd gone through the first hour of watching Kate breathe like a locomotive and wanted to crawl right out of my skin. I closed my eyes. That other nurse with the dimples wasn't wearing a ring. Maybe she'd be ready to go on a break soon.

"Excuse me."

My eyes flipped open and for a second I thought I'd died and gone to heaven. She was that gorgeous.

"Are you using this?" she asked.

She was tugging at the issue of *People* under my left thigh.

"Why? Do you need a pillow?" I said. I was waking up fast and regrouping on my charm. As she pulled the magazine away and sat down to peruse it, I sat up and checked the drool situation. And no telling how many different directions my hair was sticking up in.

"You look fine," she said dryly as she turned a page.

I grinned at her. I liked this girl. Not only did she have a great head of sandy hair and the three most perfectly placed freckles I'd ever seen on a nose, but she had that dust-me-off wit I love in a girl. No danger of her going off in giggles. I hate that. Unless, of course, she has compensating huge, hazel eyes.

I popped a Life Saver in my mouth to ward off nap breath. "Unless you've been off the planet for the last six months, you won't pick up anything new from that magazine," I said.

"I don't read much of this kind of thing," she said. "I'm usually too busy."

"I bet you are." I slid a centimeter in the direction of her chair. "I bet your social calendar looks like ..."

"I have a lot of hard classes," she said, never taking her eyes from the article on Whoopi Goldberg I'd just read three times. "And I'm really involved in my church."

"I used to be, too. Into the church thing. Now, hard classes, that's a whole other gig."

She kept reading.

"So, you're a scholar, huh?" I said.

She shrugged.

I mentally thumbed through my notes on smart girl technique. "I don't find the writing in there to be particularly good," I said.

She really looked at me for the first time, and I took that opportunity to inch closer and smile. She raised an eyebrow. I love great eyebrows in a girl.

"What do you find to be 'particularly good writing'?" she said.

"Oh, I don't know. I'm usually so into the science/math scene I don't have much time to read."

"Oh," she said.

She didn't believe me. And she was right. I like that in a girl.

But from the way she turned the page and started absorbing the words, I knew she was going to be a tough case. I glanced at my watch. *OK, Ben, challenge: Have her eating out of your hand before the baby's born.*

I got up with a sigh and moved toward the window for Technique Number One. I gazed out with all the strength-under-pressure I could muster and sighed again. Any minute now, she'd say, "You looked stressed."

She tossed the *People* onto the table and picked up a *Newsweek*. So she wasn't sensitive. I moved on to Technique Number Two.

"I could use a Coke," I said casually, moving toward the machine. "You want one?"

She shook her head, pointed to the apple juice peeking out of her tote bag, and kept reading.

I knew I'd explode if I consumed another thing, but I bought a Dr. Pepper anyway and moved on to Technique Number Three.

"I really hate to drink alone," I said.

"You obviously hate to do anything alone," she said. Her tone was annoyed but she put the magazine down. Progress.

"Today I do … with all that is going on in there …"

"All what?" she asked.

"My sister's having a baby."

"Can't you go in?"

"I guess she's having a rough time. They told me it would be better if I waited out here. Dude, it's driving me nuts."

She furrowed her eyebrows in concern, and for a minute I

thought we were getting somewhere. And then Brown Eyes sailed through.

"Your sister's doing great! Feel free to go in any time."

She swished through the glass doors, and my Challenge Girl glared at me and snatched up a *Sports Illustrated*.

It was time to skip Technique Number Four and go straight to Number Five.

"OK, so I stretched the truth a little. I was just trying to get next to you, OK? Let's start over."

She gave me a get-real look.

"So—what are you doing here? Do you have somebody in there?"

"No."

I grinned. Technique Number Five-A. "Oh. I get it. Hospital waiting rooms are the place to hang on Friday nights in Hudson. Makes sense. I mean, it beats the bowling alley."

"Don't put Hudson down unless you live here," she said.

"Does 'used to live here' count?"

"When?" she said.

"About five years ago. Then we moved to Westover."

She bit her lip and stood up.

"Look, don't go. I'm sorry if I was pushy," I said. "Please stay."

"No."

"You don't like me much, do you?" I said. That was a technique I hadn't used before. I wasn't even sure it was a technique. I really wanted to know.

She stopped halfway to the door and turned around. "Not as much as I used to," she said.

I stared at her.

"Of course, now you're so busy trying to be ... whatever, who can tell who you are?"

But I was still stuck on her first answer. "Did you know me?" I said stupidly.

"In fifth grade. Mrs. Richardson's class."

"No. You've got the wrong guy," I said.

"You're Benjie," she said. "We were in a church Christmas play together. I was Mary, you were the shepherd with the Batman bathrobe."

"Christy," I said.

As soon as I said her name, a thousand images flickered across my screen at the same time. Doing a report together on Andrew Jackson. Having a contest to see who could blow the most bubbles in their milk carton before Mrs. Richardson caught on. Riding to Sunday school with her and her parents because mine never went to church. Learning the Ten Commandments in her mother's kitchen. For a second, I could almost smell oatmeal cookies.

"You've changed," she said.

"Thank you," I said. "I was the skinniest, wimpiest kid on the planet. There is nothing adorable about an overbite."

"I liked you, Benjie." Her voice went soft. "We had so much fun back then."

"It's Ben now," I said. "Don't they call you Christina?"

"Christy. I've always been Christy. I always will be."

Two thousand dollars worth of orthodontia suddenly seemed useless. I was ten again, with weird teeth and arms the diameter of a garden hose. And Christy with the sandy hair and the fabulous freckles was seeing me as Benjie.

"We've all changed in the way we look," she was saying.

"But you're really different."

"Thank you," I said again.

But she frowned down at her hands. "I didn't mean it as a compliment," she said.

She was so sincere, and so sad, I couldn't even think of a comeback. I slouched back onto the couch.

"You didn't keep going to church after you moved, did you?" she said.

"No."

"I guess that's how it happened."

"How what happened?"

"How you got into this hitting on girls thing."

"It's not a thing. It's me."

"I don't buy that. You used to love it when my mom would say, 'Benjie, why are you so cute?' And you'd say, 'That's the way God made me, Ma.'"

"I can't believe I ever said that," I said, laughing.

"Neither can I," Christy said.

The glass doors swung open, and Dimples dimpled at me. "You're an uncle. The baby came so fast, we didn't have time to call you," she said. "Kate really wants you to join us."

My stomach began the process of turning itself inside out.

"You're an uncle," Christy said.

"Yeah, but, Dude, she's just had a baby in there ..."

Christy looked at me sadly. "Benjie would go in there and be with her."

Every soda and Life Saver I'd put in my stomach in the last three hours was making its way up my esophagus as I followed Dimples into the birthing room.

"Benjie, look!" Kate grinned at me out of a wreath of sweaty hair, and the face next to hers was tiny and red and squalling. "It's our baby!" she said.

I stared at the little human being while the rest of my family squealed into a phone somewhere in the corner.

"Am I an aunt or an uncle?" I asked. Kate guffawed.

"I mean—is it a boy or a girl?"

"It's a nephew. Garrett Benjamin. Here, you can hold him."

"Aw, no, Dude."

"You missed his birth, Ben," Kate said. "Go on, he won't break."

The little guy felt surprisingly solid as he curled into the crook of my arm. He stopped screaming and scowled into my face out of cloudy eyes.

"Isn't he beautiful?" Kate said.

"Yeah," I lied. Actually, the poor kid was wiry and wimpy and even without teeth he looked like he needed braces. But I heard myself say to him, "That's OK, Garrett. It's the way God made you."

"We're calling him Benjamin," Kate said.

I shook my head. "Nah. Call him Benjie."

"Christy said to tell you she'll see you tomorrow," Brown Eyes said to me as I was on my way out.

I almost crawled across the counter.

"Down, boy! You'll be able to catch her up here, I'm sure. She always comes up to look at the babies in the nursery."

"Always?"

"Her mom's in and out of the hospital constantly with cancer. Christy's a brave young lady."

I turned and stared through the glass into the now empty waiting room.

Ma. With cancer. And Christy hadn't even had a chance to tell me because I was so busy "hitting on her." Slowly I went for the door.

"Good night, Ben," Brown Eyes said.

I started to tell her to call me Benjie. But then I wasn't sure if I could live up to the name yet.

My Thanksgiving Buddy

"Walker? Are you depressed? You're turning down a fourth helping of mashed potatoes?"

"Leave him alone, Larry," Aunt Ev said. "Walker, have some more cranberry sauce."

"Are you depressed?" said my cousin Lydia. "You haven't said much since we sat down. Usually he talks your arm off," she said to her husband Al, newly married into the Cassinelli clan.

"When has he had a chance?" Dad said.

"And when has that ever stopped him?" Lydia said.

"Elizabeth dumped him." My little sister Julia smiled triumphantly across the table. I stabbed her with my eyes.

"I knew there was a woman involved," Larry said.

"Not a girl with much taste, obviously," Aunt Ev said. "Millie, pass Walker some more turkey."

"She didn't dump me," I said miserably. No one heard, but it was true. Elizabeth and I had never actually been going together in the first place, so how could telling me she just wanted to be friends because she was in love with Jason Lombard be termed "dumping"?

"Well, come on, unload," Lydia said. "Why'd she put you down?"

"Would you leave the poor kid alone?" said Uncle Rooney.

"This is family—spill your guts."

"Really, Lydia," said Aunt Millie. "'Spill your guts'? At the Thanksgiving dinner table?"

"Excuse me." Lydia twinkled her mischievous brown eyes at me. "Walker, do share the secrets of your poor tormented soul."

"I can share them!" Julia said cheerfully. "Elizabeth wants him to be a 'buddy,' and he wants more, and it basically means his life is over."

I choked on my sweet potatoes.

"Extension phone," Julia said smugly to the crowd.

"Bummer," Lydia said. "Do you think it could be your breath?"

"Could somebody give me a break here?" I asked.

"I'm just kidding. Have some stuffing. No, wait, it has onions in it—"

"All right, all right," Mom said. "It's time for the family tradition."

"Which one?" Uncle Rooney said.

"The one where everyone tells one thing they're thankful to God for today."

I'm thankful you changed the subject, I thought.

But as the family got semiserious, I couldn't think of anything else I was overjoyed about. I was crazy about Elizabeth, and I'd told her, and she'd replied with the I-love-you-like-a-brother speech. I could've recited it with her, I'd heard it so many times before from every girl I'd ever wanted to be more than a brother to.

"Your turn, Walker," Aunt Ev said.

I looked helplessly around the table.

"I'm thankful Julia hasn't learned to pick the lock on my room yet," I finally said.

"Just wait," Julia said.

Actually, the next morning I wished she could have picked it instead of banging on my door at 8:30.

"Walker, phone for you!" she screamed through the keyhole. "It's a girl!"

"Is it that Elizabeth person?" I heard Aunt Ev say in the hall. "I hope he plays hard to get. It would serve her right."

Other people's relatives just came for Thanksgiving dinner. Why did mine have to spend the whole weekend? Two aunts and an uncle were gathered in the kitchen when I got there. I took the phone into the pantry.

"Hello?" I said out of the smog of sleep.

"Walker? It's Elizabeth."

I was immediately wide awake. Her voice sounded like she'd been crying and was about to do it again.

"Is something wrong?"

"Everything is wrong," I think she said. She was sobbing so hard I could barely understand her.

"What's going on?"

"I need your help, or I'm afraid I'll do something really stupid."

I wasn't sure what that meant, but it scared me.

"Don't do anything stupid," I said. "Don't do anything. I'll be right there."

"OK."

"Fifteen minutes. Ten."

"Thank you."

"Liz?"

"Yeah?"

"Where's 'there'?"

"Denny's? On Wilson Street?"

"See you in five minutes," I said.

When I passed through the kitchen, they were all pretending to be involved in their scrambled eggs.

"Here, Son," Uncle Rooney said, handing me his keys. "You can use my car."

"Thanks," I said. "But I don't have a license yet."

When I got to Denny's, I was out of breath from running while donning articles of clothing. I had at least taken time to brush my teeth, just in case Lydia had been right.

Elizabeth was huddled in a booth. I didn't even have to ask what was going on before she poured out her heart between big, hiccupping sobs.

Her parents had spent all of Thanksgiving Day arguing about whether her grandmother who had Alzheimer's should go into a nursing home, and then this morning her grandmother had wandered off and been picked up by the police. So now her parents were fighting and looking for a nursing home and completely shutting *her* out.

Even with her eyes all puffy and raw, and junk coming out of her nose, she still looked like a princess.

"On top of everything," she said, "I have some problems of my own I need help with, and I can't even go to my parents with all this going on."

"What about Jason?" I asked. "Can he help you—I mean, he's your boyfriend."

"He's part of the problem."

I put my hand over hers. "Maybe you just need a day out of your house to get your head together."

"OK," she said. "But where could we go?"

I couldn't believe I was saying it, but it came out as the logical answer. "We could go to my house," I said.

I called Mom, so the Cassinelli Clan was ready for us when we got there. Mom, Aunt Millie, Aunt Ev, and Lydia were all in the kitchen making lunch—at 10 A.M. Dad, Uncle Larry, Uncle Rooney, and Al stood up when Elizabeth walked into the room, which I think was a new experience for her. Julia giggled and ran out, probably to bug the living room.

"Honey, lunch won't be ready for hours," Mom said. "Have some muffins to hold you over."

"Get her some butter and jam, Lydia," Aunt Ev said. "She's pitifully thin."

"Leave her alone, Evvie," Uncle Larry said. "Come on, Sweetheart—you like football?"

Within ten minutes Elizabeth was ensconced in the family room with a buffet in front of her, cheering Notre Dame to victory. The women cornered her after lunch and got the whole story out of her, probably with some details I hadn't even heard. I don't know; they wouldn't let me into the kitchen.

"We'll all be praying for you," I heard Aunt Millie say. "The Lord won't abandon you."

I finally had her to myself when all the men conked out in front of the third game and the women went out shopping. They wanted to take Elizabeth with them, but I talked them into taking Julia instead.

We sat in the living room in the window seat with a fire

going, and she settled back into the cushions and sighed like the problems of a thousand years were easing out of her.

"Are you feeling better?" I said.

"A lot. This has been a great day—only, it doesn't really change what's going on at my house. I wish my family were like yours."

"They're pretty bizarre."

"I still don't know what to do about everything, but I feel like I can at least go home now and face it again. Thanks for being there for me."

She looked at me with tears in her eyes. All I could do was smile like a dork.

* * * * *

Julia screeched in while we were all still at the lunch table on Saturday. "Elizabeth's here!" she yelled.

Half the table got up to peer out the window.

"Ooh—she has a package," Aunt Millie said.

"God bless her," Aunt Ev said.

"Walker, don't be a dolt—get the door," Uncle Rooney said.

"Stay here, Walker, I'll go!" Julia said.

"Leave him alone!" said the entire kitchen.

Lydia squeezed my arm as I elbowed my way out. "Good luck, Big Guy," she said.

As soon as I saw Elizabeth, I forgot that my whole family probably had their ears pressed to the kitchen door. Her eyes were clear and sparkly again and she was smiling as only Princess Elizabeth could.

"Come on in," I said. "How are things going?"

"Better. My parents thought I was crazy when I told them I thought we ought to start praying like your family does, but at least nobody's screaming at each other today."

"There's something to be said for that," I said.

"Walker?" she said.

I could hardly breathe.

"I know it's going to take a long time for things to really change at my house, and maybe they never will. But whenever I get that feeling like I have to get out, can I come over here?"

"Anytime. And listen, all these people don't always live here."

"They're sweet. I'll miss them. Oh." She put the package into my hands. "This is for you. It's a tape—Christian rock—I thought you might ..."

"You didn't have to do this," I said. "I just helped you because I care about you."

"I know you do," she said. "You are the best friend—the best brother—anyone could have." She kissed me on the cheek. "Promise me you'll always be my buddy."

After I walked her out, I couldn't face the interrogation in the kitchen so I went into the garage and sat on top of a pile of sleeping bags and shivered. I was miserable anyway, so it didn't matter.

I was going over the phrase, "Promise you'll always be my buddy" for the hundredth time when Lydia joined me and handed me a piece of pumpkin pie.

"When depressed, eat something fattening," she said.

"Thanks." I stuffed a large forkful into my mouth and chewed gloomily.

"You got the 'friends' thing again, huh?" she said.

"Yeah."

"Look, Walker, I know I've been riding you pretty hard, but

let me tell you something—I mean, seriously."

"Do I have a choice?" I asked.

"This is a three-parter. First—A friend is exactly what Elizabeth needs right now, and you're being that for her. From what I gather, her boyfriend's a jerk and doesn't give her half what you do. If you really care about her, that should make you happy."

"You're serious, huh?" I said. I put the fork down and listened.

"Second—If you were more to her than a friend, your life would get very complicated. She'd be going to somebody else to get advice about you.

"Now—third—What you're doing right now is preparing yourself for some girl to really fall hard for you."

"Right. They're standing in line."

"They aren't at this moment. But when they get to be my age—hey, a whole twenty-five—they're going to want a guy to love who also knows how to be a friend to them." She pointed to my piecrust.

"Are you going to eat that?"

I shook my head.

"You know how adults say not to get so involved when you're a teenager?" she said, munching.

"No one ever had to say that to me," I said.

"The point is, you're doing it the right way. God's way. It's gonna pay off, trust me."

And even though she said it with a lip full of whipped cream, I did.

We all went to church together Sunday morning.

Uncle Rooney, Uncle Larry, and Dad harmonized on the

hymns. Too bad they were in the wrong key.

Aunt Millie, Aunt Ev, and Mom all cried during the sermon. Who knows why? They also shared one Kleenex through the whole ordeal. Julia giggled, and Lydia kept nudging us with her elbows—me on one side and her husband Al on the other.

Me? I sat there thanking God for all the things I couldn't think of at the dinner table Thanksgiving Day. For more food than even I could eat. For a noisy, bizarre, totally unselfish family. And for the chance to be Elizabeth's friend.

They all left for their own homes after church—and I was actually sorry to see them go.

The Girl's Totally Changed

That's her, McCann," Marcus said to me for the third time.

"It can't be," I said. "She moved away—right before sophomore year."

Marcus slid a Hershey bar across the counter to a kid and took his money, but he never stopped shaking his head. "I'm telling you, Jeff, she's come back to visit her cousin, Mimi What's-Her-Face. Her parents got divorced after they moved. Her mother is freaking out and she sent her here." Marcus vaulted over the counter. "The show's starting. I'll get the doors."

I swept up the popcorn, but my mind was on the girl in the very short skirt, wearing enough makeup for two girls. She'd come into the theatre ten minutes earlier with a crowd who all had their lips curled like they were just *waiting* for somebody to tell them how trampy they were. That girl *couldn't* have been Kim.

When we were in the seventh grade, Kim Lindsey was my Juliet—and I was her Romeo. She was Guinevere, and I was—well, you get the idea.

I could still remember us sitting in church together and me

realizing—hey—cool—we're gonna spend eternity together. Even after I broke up with her over who-knows-what—I mean, you can be pretty clueless in seventh grade—I'd sometimes get this twinge when I saw her, because she was my first "real" girl-friend. We'd "gone out" for all of two months, but that was for-ever in middle school.

I slid some loose ice under the ice machine with my foot and leaned on the broom. If Marcus was right and it was her—nah, it couldn't be. She had been the wholesome type you saw on the covers of Christian teen magazines. Straight As. No moods. Just always a smile. No way that chick with the broody face had been *my* Kim.

"It's her all right!" Marcus banged the swinging door against the wall, coming into the lobby. "I went down to tell her cousin and those other girls to shut up, and I saw it was Kim Lindsey for sure. Man, has she changed. Bad news, McCann. I'd give her a real wide margin."

I shrugged for his benefit, but I suddenly had other ideas. After all, Romeo never gave up on Juliet.

When the movie was over and the crowd belched out, I held the door open. "Hi, Kim," I said with a grin when she blinked into the lobby. "Remember me?"

"Oh, yeah," she said, looking around her with an uneasy smile plastered on with lip gloss.

"Good to see you," I said.

Nothing.

"Want to meet me for a Coke?"

Shrug.

"I'll meet you at the Red & White as soon as I get off."

She muttered something. I wasn't sure if, by the time I

scraped all the obvious gum off the floor, she'd even be there, but the more I thought about it, the more I had to give it a shot. I mean, if I wasn't Romeo or Lancelot, at least I was a Christian.

"You're losing it, McCann," Marcus told me as I went out the door.

I was surprised that she was at a table, alone, arms jammed into a fold across her chest, five earrings twinkling from each ear and one from her nose. Had to be a sign that she really wanted to be the person she used to be—or that she still was.

"Hi," I said.

"Hi."

"I didn't know you were back in Quincy."

She finally looked at me. "You didn't even know I left."

"Sure I did." I straddled a chair and tried to look casual.

"Look ..." She sighed and rolled her eyes the way girls do when teachers yell at them. "Let's just get this over with, OK? Yes, my parents got a divorce. Yes, my mother almost had a nervous breakdown. And yes, she shipped me here to Mimi's so I could 'get my head together.'"

I tried to keep the smile on my face, but I knew it was looking kind of like a Popsicle.

"You can leave if you want," she said.

Although her eyes were better guarded than Folsom Prison, for a tenth of a second I saw some Kim-ness in them. *Come on, Romeo,* I told myself. *This was Juliet.*

I sucked in some air. "Listen, I'm sorry about everything that's ... happened to you. You must really hurt."

She snorted. She actually snorted. "How would you know? You come from the perfect little family. You're probably still on the honor roll. You have the cute little job in the Old Town Theatre so you can save up for college. Nothing's changed for you."

I fumbled around for something—anything—to say. "Are you still mad at me for breaking up with you?"

She let her lower jaw drop. "Three years ago? In junior high? Get real."

"Then why are you acting like you're ticked off at me?"

She picked up the salt shaker and examined it carefully. "My shrink says I'm just mad at everybody. Nobody understands how I feel, so I get mad and then they really don't understand and then I don't have to deal with them because they run away."

Her shrink? Whoa. Maybe this hero thing was a little more involved than it looked like on stage.

But there was that little bit of Kim-ness in her eyes—and that big load of ego in me.

"I *don't* understand," I said. "But I can try to."

Her lip curled up almost to the nose ring. "Why?" she said.

"Because … you were my first girlfriend."

I saw an almost-smile playing at the corners of her mouth. "You were my first boyfriend." She gave what I think was a laugh. "So, why'd you break up with me, you jerk?"

"'Cause—I was an idiot."

I could hear Marcus agreeing. But maybe we were getting somewhere. She was responding. I might even be helping her.

I said the next thing that came into my head.

"We've got a thing Saturday up at Gray Eagle Camp—all the old kids you knew in junior high. You want to go with me?"

The smile disappeared. "I'm sure they'll all be thrilled to see me."

"Come on. It should be cool."

She rolled her eyes, but I think she nodded.

* * * * *

"I still don't get why you brought her," Marcus said on Saturday as we unloaded ice chests out of the van belonging to Pete, our youth leader.

He nodded his head toward where Kim was standing, wearing the shortest shorts on the planet, arms crossed over a cut-off-at-the-midriff T-shirt that read—well, never mind what it read.

"She just needs somebody to care about her again," I said.

"Somebody? You mean you?" Marcus said.

"Maybe."

"If you want to do an experiment, enter the science fair."

I actually had pretty high hopes when I headed toward Kim with a Sprite, and I wasn't even that disappointed when my invitation to play volleyball met with a pair of rolling eyes and more crossed arms. She never *had* been big on sports.

So while everybody else started a game, I sat on the sidelines and listened to her sigh.

It should have gone into the Guinness Book of World Records for being the longest volleyball game in youth group history. I alternated between wishing I were out there spiking, asking Kim questions she didn't answer, and telling her jokes she didn't laugh at.

"You feel weird being back with all the kids you used to know, huh?" I said finally.

"They're all staring at me."

That was true. All but Marcus, who was staring at me.

"You *have* changed," I said. "But only on the outside. They just hafta get to know you again."

She gave me another disgusted look, but the flicker was there again, like she *wanted* to believe me. So even though she picked at a burger bun all through the barbecue and never opened her mouth while we were singing with Pete's guitar, I had hopes.

"Ready to give up yet?" Marcus hissed to me at the ice chest.

"I'm making progress," I said.

He grunted.

When a chill hit the air and Pete got a fire going, he told all of us to snuggle in. "We're going to go around the circle," he said, "and you can each share how you knew God was with you today—even if it was just because Marcus remembered to bring the ice."

While everyone snickered, he looked at Kim and said quietly, "Nobody *has* to do this."

But of course everybody did it. We'd been doing this kind of thing in youth group since we were all in the seventh grade. Kim had once been really good at it.

Still, it didn't surprise me that she stiffened up like a tube of dry glue beside me. I looked at Marcus, who pantomimed slitting his throat from across the circle.

When it was my turn, I grinned at Kim. "I knew God was with me today," I said, "because Kim was back with us."

It got quiet. Pete nodded until I thought his head was going to come off. Somebody else gave a halfhearted "yea."

"Do you want to give it a go, Kim?" Pete asked.

She looked around wildly at all of us—and then she just got up and took off.

As I rushed off after her, I could hear Marcus playing taps with his lips.

I didn't catch her until she was at the pay phone at the Country Store, trying to dig change out of a pocket she could barely get her hand into.

"Kim …"

"Don't say anything, OK? Just don't say anything."

"We don't have to hang around with the youth group, OK? We can do this, just you and me."

"No!" She pulled out a dime, swore, and pitched it into the dirt. "The other day, at the Red & White, I thought maybe I could be the good little girl again if somebody like you was around—but my life got messed up, OK? You don't even know the half of it. Being around all these kids again makes me see that I am different—permanently different. I wear different clothes. I swear. Don't be shocked, OK, but I don't believe in God anymore!" She gave a mock gasp—but there were tears in her eyes. "You can't change me back to the way I used to be."

Like the dope I was in seventh grade, I just stood there. Romeo had long since disappeared.

She'd managed to extricate a quarter by then and with shaking fingers was putting it into the phone.

"What are you doing?" I said.

"Calling Mimi. They'll come get me. Just go back, OK? Please?"

Only because it was the first sincere thing she'd said since she'd come back did I just nod and leave her there.

Marcus found me later in Pete's car.

"Say 'I told you so' and you're dead meat," I said.

"I'm not going to say anything," he said. And he didn't. In

fact, he never mentioned her again. He knew Romeo was gone, too.

* * * * *

I saw Kim get on the bus the day she left town at the end of the summer. I hadn't stopped thinking about her, really, even though I'd stopped thinking I could "save" her. But seeing her with her one-way ticket in her hand and her jeans hanging down past her belly button made me realize something.

If I'd met her for the first time that day in the theatre, I'd never even have said hi to her. But I was going to keep on thinking about her, maybe even praying for her, because she was my first Juliet—and somewhere in my mind, she always would be.